Recovering Hope

By

USA Today Bestselling Author

MARION UECKERMANN

PRAISE FOR *Recovering Hope*

Very few books draw the reader in and grab the reader's emotions like *Recovering Hope* does! A very powerful book with a gripping tale of deep loss and sorrow, feeling abandoned and even hated by God, fighting one's way back from the depths of despair to having faith restored, and finding God had a purpose greater than they thought possible. A truly emotional read that will touch one's heart long after the last page and encourage the reader that God will never abandon us, even while going through dark valleys.

~ Becky Smith

Oh, my! The rollercoaster ride of emotions I experienced left me breathless. As Hope and Tyler go through what will probably be the most difficult time in their lives, we feel their angst, their pain, their plunge to the depths, and finally their joy. *Recovering Hope* will leave you with a renewed faith in God as we come to realize that God is there all the time, no matter what we go through. A highly recommended read you will remember for years to come.

~ Jan Elder, Author of Love, Lies, and Fireflies

Reading, for me, has always been a great love. You can travel to places I would never get to any other way; you can find humor and literally laugh out loud when no other person is around you. You can learn about history, sports, maybe science....the world is at your fingertips when you love to read! Every now and then you may come across a book that simply grabs your heart strings and carries you along for a ride. *Recovering Hope* is such a book. It has happy moments, joyful celebrations, beautiful characters....and heartbreaking despair. Yes, I said despair.

Recovering Hope is a book that gives you all of these things and more...it also gives you HOPE. Hope for a future when your whole world is crashing down around you. Hope that someday, no matter what has happened, there will be light in your life again. Hope that resonates throughout your soul that there IS a God, and that He does love us. I always say that God has a plan and a reason for everything, even if we cannot see it at the time, one day we will have something so wonderful happen in our lives and realize that we would never be in this exact moment if that crushing situation had not taken place. *Recovering Hope* is that story....please read and be ready to cry....and rejoice!

~ Paula Marie, Blogger and Book Reviewer at Fiction Full of Faith

Tyler and Hope's story will touch your heart. We all suffer loss and ask hard questions at some point in our lives. Without minimizing the heartache, this book offers hope and encouragement that 'if we can't see His hand, we can trust His heart'.

~ Ailsa Williams, Editor

Y'all, I don't think I've shed so many tears as I have reading Hope and Tyler's story! A story of pure happiness transpiring into total devastation all while God is hanging on every detail and brings forth His strength, love, and courage to pour into the characters' hearts. Bringing to us a story full of emotion that in some way we all can relate to.

Hope and Tyler share a love that is tested beyond something so horrific that no one should ever go through. Will they lean on each other so they can overcome this horrific tragedy? God's love they have in their hearts and lives is put to the test, just as it is for us sometimes.

Read with me this powerful testimony of how God is always with us, and He will never forsake us—that we all can overcome the most horrific battle we could ever face, with complete love and trust in our Father.

Marion has poured heart and soul into this story and the characters. A story that will change lives everywhere!

~ Sharon Dean

God never allows anything to be purposeless, neither the triumphs nor the tragedies. But when we are in the middle of either triumph or tragedy, it is hard to see the big plan. Occasionally, God lets us see after the fact what He had in mind in the first place. All of which is a demonstration of His love for people

As we journey with Hope and Tyler, we follow their entire path, up, down, and sideways. It's a journey not to be missed. If the purpose of fiction is to provide the reader with a powerful emotional experience, Marion has accomplished that beautifully, emphasizing love in the process. You won't want to miss *Recovering Hope.*

~ Judith Robl, Author *As Grandma Says*

Tears were present through much of this book as Tyler and Hope spent a year overcoming a great tragedy. We see God's love and healing throughout. The story line was emotional, filled with vivid characters. This book is recommended for those who love Christian romance with a strong inspirational message.

~ Linda Rainey

Sometimes life events are so painful and overpowering, that you lose hope. You try everything to numb the pain, all because it hurts too much to face the pain. Throughout this book I kept thinking, would I want to just end my life, or would I reach out to Jesus and draw my strength from Him? Is my faith strong enough to get me through the pain?

Oh, the deep emotions I experienced while reading this book!

Tyler and Hope's life together was very relatable and full of young love. Unfortunately, their world came crashing down one day and it took everything for them to find stable ground to stand on.

Now, I've had babies, yet I've never lost one. I can only imagine it must be a very devastating loss to experience. However, I do relate to the overwhelming issues of depression. Our family walked through a time when one of our children felt suicide was the only answer. God had His hand in getting our child the help she needed, and we truly praise Him now as we look back on all He did for us during that time.

I want to thank the author, Marion Ueckermann—she has a beautiful way of blending words together. This story was well written and flowed smoothly, so smooth that at the end my heart was tumbling all over the place. I cried throughout this book. *Recovering Hope* touched my heart so deeply, that I know it will stay with me for a long time.

One question brought out in this story is, "Can you trust God with your pain? Can you say, like Job, 'though He slay me, yet will I hope in Him'?"

The most important lesson I learned is to find my hope in God and His unending love for me.

~ Marylin Furumasu, MF Literary Works

Marion Ueckermann's unique writing style has this avid reader always coming back for another inspiring page turning read. First, I appreciate the author's attention to details. Her research into oceanography, customs, the Hawaiian language and American word choice is impeccable. Second, the subtle allusions to Biblical pregnancies touched this mother's heart. Third, the word play in the title made me ponder the meaning of hope in my life, as well as *Restoring Hope*, the character and/or restoring hope for others. Fourth, the interpretation of spiritual truths had me rereading Job's story—the Lord gives and the Lord takes away; may His name be praised forever. Finally, being married for 45 years, I can relate to Hope and Tyler as a couple. My husband also likes to contemplate every aspect of a situation, discusses each aspect in great detail, before making a decision. Hope and I would be friends. A well-crafted, emotional story of heartbreak and loss.

~ Renate Pennington, Retired English, Journalism, Creative Writing High School Teacher

Restoring Hope may be the most personal fiction book I have ever read. This author takes a highly sensitive subject and bares the recovery process for all to see. She did not shy away from the tough moments and I truly believe that this book will help women in their healing process. This story shows great compassion and evokes many emotions. Make sure you have a box of tissues.

~ Joelle Teague

Marion Ueckermann grabs a hold of our emotions from the get-go in this powerful story. A story of guilt, forgiveness, and second chances.

We often learn lessons in unexpected places.

Hope and Tyler suffer a loss. They both learn things from their jobs to help them deal with life and each other. Tyler has a project that teaches patience and persistence. Hope works with dolphins and one teaches her strength and hope. Through it all, Marion imparts God's love and grace to us all.

~ Renette Steele

Dear Reader

Bad things happen.
To good people.
Sometimes the purpose is made known.
Most times we never figure out the why.
But God knows.
And that's all that matters.

May you know His perfect peace as you traverse the valleys of life.

Be blessed,

Marion

To Jessica ~

who smiles through the dark

He has sent me
to bind up the brokenhearted,
to proclaim freedom for the captives
and release from darkness for the prisoners,
...to comfort all who mourn,
and provide for those who grieve in Zion—
to bestow on them a crown of beauty
instead of ashes,
the oil of joy
instead of mourning,
and a garment of praise
instead of a spirit of despair.

~ Isaiah 61:1-3 (NIV)

CHAPTER ONE

Friday, September 14, 2001

STANDING IN their bathroom in front of his wife, Hope, Tyler Peterson tried to sneak a peek over her shoulder. Way beyond excited, Tropical Storm Gabrielle had nothing on the churning in his gut.

His pulse skipped a beat at Hope's squeal as she pushed a palm against his face, shoving his wayward gaze away. "Tyler, no! We're supposed to look at the results together. And the test states three to four minutes. Barely one has passed since I peed on the stick."

"Aw, honey…"

Yesterday they'd scurried about purchasing supplies in preparation for the storm. But he'd only just found out that Hope had done a little secret shopping of her own. At the pharmacy.

Today, his world could be turned upside down. Just like his home state. From the television in the living room, an early morning newscast filtered through the one-bedroomed apartment reporting that Gabrielle had struck Venice, forty-eight miles south of Clearwater where they lived. They felt some of the effects as the wind blustered outside and rain pelted against the windows of his and Hope's little tenth-floor love nest. The storm had definitely intensified overnight.

As if they needed another storm in their lives with the country reeling from the terrorist attacks on the Pentagon and the Twin Towers, just three days earlier. Now, their part of the world had to deal with an attack from nature as well.

Standing in their bathroom in front of his wife, unable to contain his excitement, despite what was happening around them, Tyler tried to sneak a peek over her shoulder.

Hope cupped his bristled jaw, then brushed her lips across his and whispered, "Patience, my love. Patience."

Tyler squared his shoulders. "I *am* a patient man. A resilient one too." His arms lovingly circled her waist.

Head thrown back, her long, dark hair tickling his fingers, Hope's laughter floated toward the ceiling. "*Ku'uipo*, with my family, you had to be. They really put you through the wringer when we started dating."

Tyler smoothed a hand over her straight, silky hair then tucked a thick lock behind one ear. He loved it when Hope used terms of endearment in her native tongue. Sweetheart was by far one of his favorites, and she knew it. He'd told her once it sounded like cupid. She'd replied that although the word didn't mean cupid, he'd definitely shot his arrow of love right through her heart.

How he adored this woman. He'd do anything for her, go through anything for her—even stand up to an overbearing, overprotective family.

Giving a slight shrug, he chuckled. "They certainly did. Every single one of them. Your parents, brothers, uncles, aunts, cousins… Even your friends."

Hope pinched his cheek, offering him a mischievous grin.

2

"That's what you get when you date a girl from Hawaii. When it comes to family values, we're old-fashioned, and we look out for each other."

She pressed her body close against his, her breath warm in his neck.

Tyler's pulse raced, and his breathing quickened. If the pregnancy test turned out negative, they could always spend the day trying again to make a baby. After all, they weren't going anywhere in this weather.

Hope leaned back, breaking his train of thought as she said, "But you persevered, and by the time you asked for permission to marry me, my family and friends were all as crazy as I was about the all-American boy who shared my love, and theirs, for *ka moana*."

The ocean… What wasn't to love? It was fascinating, deep, and beautiful—just like Hope. How strange that a guy who grew up at the foot of the Rocky Mountains should have such a passion for the wild blue yonder. But now he could see it was all part of God's incredible plan for his life. If he hadn't been so drawn to the sea, he would never have studied to be a marine engineer, never have met his wife while working on assignment in Honolulu. And never have rededicated his life to Christ during that church picnic at Fort DeRussy Park beside Waikiki Beach.

He'd spent that day hanging out with Hope, playing beach volleyball—on opposing teams—and swimming together in the ocean. After everyone had gone home, Hope had agreed to go snorkeling with him on the reef at San Souci Beach, a little farther south. That was the first of many sunsets they'd since enjoyed together. What a day it had been—a new beginning in his spiritual life *and* his love life.

Pushing aside his musing, Tyler asked, "Have you told your family of your suspicions yet?"

She shook her head. "I'd never spill the beans on something as big as this before telling you. Besides, I don't want to say anything to anyone until we're past the first trimester. All right?"

First trimester? Pregnancy certainly came with an entirely different vocabulary, one he was possibly about to embark on learning.

New language aside, he couldn't understand Hope's hesitancy to broadcast the best news ever, should it come. If they were about to become parents, he wanted to rush out and tell the entire world. And if *his* parents were still alive, they'd be the first to know.

Well, perhaps Hope could keep it from her family, but how on earth would he keep news like this from his siblings for several weeks? Faith and Brody would want to know, just as he'd known the moment Faith became pregnant with Michael, and Brody's wife, Madison, with their daughter, Charity. He prayed he wouldn't follow in his brother and sister's footsteps of raising one-child families. He wanted at least three, like their family had been, although four would be a better number because there'd be no middle child. Faith had complained that being the second of three, she'd often felt a little excluded. Brody, as the oldest, had been more prone to receiving privileges and responsibilities, and as the youngest, Tyler had been indulged. So, if he could help it, there'd be no place for middle child syndrome in their home.

Hope checked the time on her wristwatch and smiled. "Three minutes. Are you ready?"

"On three?"

She nodded and they chorused together, "One. Two. Three…"

Hope swung around and Tyler quickly moved to her side. Two blue lines on the indicator trumpeted the truth. They were pregnant!

Sweeping her up in his arms, Tyler twirled Hope around. "We're going to have a baby!"

Tears welled in her dark brown eyes. "I can't believe it—I'm *hāpai!*"

"I'm happy, too."

A laugh bubbled past Hope's lips. "Oh, now there's a word you haven't had the need to learn yet. Yes, I am happy, but *hāpai* means pregnant."

Chuckling at his blunder, Tyler set Hope down on her feet again. He snatched up the pregnancy test and held it in front of her. Might as well have a little more fun. The occasion called for it.

"Actually, we're going to have two babies. Boys."

With a giggle, Hope quirked one perfect brow. "Really? And you know that how?"

"Two blue stripes, that's how, my love."

She smacked his shoulder lightly. "You're such a tease, Tyler. That's the positive result. And I already explained that to you. One stripe would've been negative, remember? As for the color of the stripes—determined purely by the manufacturer. I could've chosen a test that showed pink stripes. What would you have thought then? Would you have been as ecstatic to have a little Hope?"

Tyler made a buzzer sound. "Busted. But jokes aside…pink, blue, it doesn't matter to me, although a little hope is always a good thing. All that's of consequence, honey, is that we're going to be *he'ohana.*" Yes, he'd picked up more than a few Hawaiian words during the two years since he and Hope had met, and he relished any opportunity to use them. But he probably did need to expand his vocabulary. Especially as Hope would surely want to teach their children the language she'd grown up with.

"A family… Yes." Uncertainty clouded Hope's face. "So, it *really* doesn't matter to you whether we have a boy or a girl?"

Tyler shook his head. "Not a bit. As long as he or she is healthy, with ten fingers and ten toes. And even if our baby has more than the standard ten tootsies, I'd still love it." He'd heard of babies being born with eleven toes.

Her eyes brightened. "Really?"

Tyler drew Hope into a kiss, reassuring her how little it mattered whether they had a son or a daughter. Finally releasing her, his gaze searched hers. He cracked a grin. "I guess we'll need a bigger apartment."

"Better still, a house. With a garden." Her lips curved into a beautiful smile.

"I like that idea. And it is time."

"B–but we can still stay here a few months longer. Save some money."

Tyler nodded. "We can. And we will. However, we shouldn't let that deter us from house-hunting. It could take a while to find the perfect place. And then the transfer of the property will take some time too, I guess."

Shifting his gaze to the shelf beside the basin and the second pregnancy test Hope had bought—just in case the first test was negative because it was taken too early—Tyler said, "I guess we don't need this now."

He lifted the box to check the expiration date. "This test's different to the one you just took."

She giggled. "I wasn't sure which would be the best test, so I took two different brands."

"Well, it's still good until July 2004."

Hope took the box from him and set it back down on the shelf. "I'll pack it away later. Never know when we might need another one in a hurry."

"Yep, you never know." Tyler waggled his brows.

Taking Hope's hand, he led her out of the bathroom into their bedroom. "What do you say we first give thanks to our Father for this precious gift of life? Afterwards, we can surf the net for properties. Not much else to do—it isn't fit outside for man or beast."

"I'd like that."

Tyler knelt in front of their bed.

Hope settled down on her knees beside him. "Are we going to survive this, *ko'u aloha*?" Concern creased her brow.

He flashed her a smile. "Of course we are. We're not the first people to become parents. Many have survived before us, and many will survive after us. Just think, twenty-one months ago, the world faced Y2K, the Millennium bug, and got through it. Now our nation has been rocked by 911, but we will overcome that too. Soon, we'll face Gen Z, our own little millennial bug. But with each other to lean on, we'll get through the changes this will bring in our lives. I can't wait to face each challenge with you by my side."

Had he managed to reassure Hope? Allay any fears she suddenly seemed to have?

He could only try his best to support her where possible and leave the rest to God. After all, he wasn't the one who was pregnant. It was Hope's body that would change in the coming months. And along with those changes, there'd no doubt be challenges too.

Time to up his game from fabulous hubby to super hubby.

CHAPTER TWO

LIKE CLOCKWORK, Hope threw back the covers and shot out of bed. She sprinted for the bathroom, praying she'd make it there on time. She'd had to mop up vomit more than once the past two weeks. At least, Tyler had, poor thing. While she'd clung to the toilet bowl, he'd dutifully filled a bucket with soapy water and cleaned up after her. What an amazing husband—she would never be able to survive her pregnancy without him. How on earth did single moms manage to do this alone?

Tyler rushed into the bathroom after her as she slid to her knees and clutched the toilet bowl.

"You okay, honey?" He wet a facecloth then handed it to her.

The cool freshness of the damp terry cloth against her face always made her feel a little better. Leaning back on her heels, Hope pulled the cloth from her face and released a long groan toward the ceiling. "How long will this go on?"

Tyler knelt down on the floor beside her and wrapped her in his embrace. "I wish I could take this from you. I'd gladly bear the morning nausea on your behalf if it were possible."

Hope forced a smile to her face as she stared at his bed head, tufts of dark hair flying this way and that. "You just continue doing what it is you do best...making those little underwater robots of yours for marine research and being an awesome husband."

Trailing a finger across her cheek, Tyler's dark gaze searched hers. "Did you ask Doctor Phillips about it yesterday?"

She offered Tyler a slow nod. "He said it should pass by the time I enter the second trimester and that at least it's not HG."

A frown rippled Tyler's brow. "HG? Heavy gas?"

Hope gave him a weak smack against his arm. "No, silly. *Hyperemesis Gravidarum*. If it were, you would probably have had to admit me by now for intravenous fluids and feeding. HG lasts all day and often doesn't go away for the entire nine months, so I'm really thankful that I only feel sick first thing in the morning."

"Well, I'm thankful too that things aren't that bad." Tyler rose then helped Hope to her feet. "You're awfully pale today, honey. Why don't you stay in bed—take a sick day? It's almost the weekend. Surely the rescue center can do without you for eight hours?"

"I can't. We've got routine preventative health procedures planned on the dolphins. I'm needed there." Hope crept back into bed. "But first, just let me lie down for a little longer. I promise if I don't feel well, I'll come home as soon as I'm done."

"You don't need to go *into* the tank, do you?" Concern laced Tyler's words.

Hope shook her head. "No. And I wouldn't either. My days of squeezing into scuba gear are over until this baby is born. Besides, soon I won't be able to fit into a wetsuit. I'm already delegating any tasks requiring breathing in compressed air."

"Good. You need to take care, my little marine vet. You're responsible for another life now, not just your beloved sea creatures."

Hope scrunched her nose. "I know."

9

Bending forward, Tyler kissed her on the forehead. He smiled. "Rest while I make you a cup of ginger tea with a side of crackers."

"Thank you, *ku'uipo*. You're the best."

Tyler exited the bedroom, soon returning with Hope's standard breakfast these days. Gosh, she missed wolfing down a plate of bacon and eggs.

Bile rushed up her throat again. *Oops, shouldn't have thought that.*

Taking a deep breath, she shimmied up in bed and instantly reached for the cracker. As she bit into the saltine, Tyler set the empty plate and cup of tea down on the bedside pedestal. Once she got the tea and the dry cracker into her stomach, she'd be able to get up and get dressed.

Tyler sank onto the mattress beside her. "Honey, I've been thinking… Maybe you should consider giving up work now already."

Hope nearly choked on her cracker. She quickly swallowed. "What? You've got to be joking. I love my job, and I'll work for as long as I possibly can."

That was a bit harsh, and uncalled for. And totally not Ephesians five…wanting her own way instead of submitting to her husband. Tyler was just being his usual caring self. She hadn't needed to bite his head off. Probably these pregnancy hormones invading her body.

"I–I'm just concerned about the wet pavements at the aquarium. You could slip and fall. Or you could get bumped in the stomach by a dolphin or a manatee. Any number of things could go wrong that could hurt the baby."

"As they could here at home. Tyler, I can't wrap myself in cotton wool." Too harsh, again.

She brushed her hand up and down his forearm and offered him a smile. "I'll be fine. I promise I'll do everything I can to be careful. I know I'm carrying precious cargo."

Two hours later, Hope pulled her black Jeep Wrangler to a halt outside the marine rescue center. Tropical Storm Gabrielle a thing of the past, the sun shone down gloriously from azure skies.

Hope swept her hair up between her fingers and tied it in a high ponytail with an elastic band. Dressed in her royal blue work T-shirt, black shorts, and sturdy, waterproof sandals, she was ready for another day working at the job she loved so much.

A knot formed in her stomach, uncertainty threatening her peace. Would motherhood satisfy her in the same way?

Pushing aside the negative thought, she slid out of the car and headed inside.

From beside one of the large pools, Sandy, the dolphin trainer, waved. The pretty twenty-five-year-old brunette smiled as Hope neared. "Good morning. We're just about ready for you." She raised her hands in the air and gave three claps.

Two gray forms glided through the water toward them.

Benny and Joon, their bottlenose dolphins.

Benny, the oldest, had been rescued twelve years ago when the five month old calf had been found alone and malnourished near Gullivan Bay. It was not known what had become of his mother.

Four years later, a female orphaned calf was rescued and brought to the aquarium after her mother had beached in Tampa Bay and died. Hot on the release of the romantic comedy movie *Benny & Joon*, the new arrival's name was a given.

Neither Benny nor Joon were candidates for release because they hadn't learned the necessary survival skills from their mothers for life in the deep sea.

Sandy knelt down on the thin spongy mat that covered the

platform overhanging the pool.

The dolphins came to an abrupt stop sending a wave of water under the platform. They rested their heads on the edge and Sandy rubbed her hands over their snouts as she greeted them.

"Sorry I'm late." Ethan, Hope's intern, hurried closer, the stethoscope around his neck swaying with each step. In one hand he clutched the portable ultrasound machine, and in the other he held an ophthalmoscope for the eye exam.

Hope chuckled. "Oversleep again, Ethan?"

He shrugged. "Something like that. I was up late, studying. Final year...got to nail it."

Ethan eased onto his knees beside Sandy and opened the ultrasound machine. He untangled the stethoscope from his neck and handed the device to Hope.

"You keep this up and you're going to know more than I do." Hope flashed Ethan a grin. "You need a girlfriend. Or a wife. There's more to life than just studying, studying, studying."

Sandy giggled, eyeing Ethan as she gently pushed the larger male dolphin away from the edge, back into the pool. Then she glided Joon into a horizontal position beside the platform, holding the female in position by the tail.

Hope listened to Joon's heart, lungs, and other organs with the stethoscope. "No problems detected." She picked up the ophthalmoscope and examined Joon's left eye, then easing the dolphin's head onto the edge of the platform, she checked the right eye.

Joon stretched her head forward and rubbed her nose against Hope's stomach, emitting a buzzing sound.

Laughing, Hope glanced at Ethan and Sandy. Both had raised a brow.

Uh-oh, had Joon detected her baby's heartbeat with her concentrated echolocation and let the proverbial cat out of the bag?

Of course, the theory of dolphins detecting pregnancy in humans had never been proven, still maybe Joon's actions were proof.

Sandy's breath hitched. "Are you—?"

"Ultrasound, Ethan. Please." Hope shot a prayer to heaven that by the time she'd finished scanning Joon's internal organs, her colleagues would've forgotten the little interaction that had just happened with the female dolphin.

At Sandy's guidance, Joon flipped over onto her stomach, allowing Hope to run the transducer probe over her smooth, rubbery skin. Hearing a second, faint heartbeat, Hope's eyes widened.

Well I never... What were the odds?

Ethan pointed at the monitor and stuttered, "Is t–that a—?"

Sandy leaned forward to peek at the screen. She let out a loud squeal. "Joon's going to be a mamma?"

Hope couldn't help grinning. "Looks like it." She rubbed the dolphin's belly.

Joon rolled over then disappeared beneath the water, coming up seconds later. Her body vertical to the water, she bounced her head up and down, producing a burst of clicking sounds. She seemed as excited as they were.

Sandy snapped her head to Hope. "Speaking of pregnancies... Is there something you want to tell us?" Her gaze dropped to Hope's middle.

Hope grinned.

Ethan's eyes widened. "No way... Seriously? Is that why you had me doing all the scuba activities these past two weeks?"

Finger to her mouth, Hope shushed them. "Please, don't say anything to anyone just yet. Tyler and I are keeping it quiet until I'm passed the first trimester."

CHAPTER THREE

RISING FROM her bed, stomach tangled in a knot, Hope waited for the urge to run and greet the porcelain bowl, a ritual she'd become so familiar with since her pregnancy was confirmed. Seven weeks of retching every morning hadn't been fun. Oh, she loved being pregnant, but she did not love the morning sickness.

She waited, anxious.

Nothing.

She felt perfectly normal. Absolutely zero nausea.

Could it be…?

She pulled her robe on over her pajamas, shoved her feet into her slippers, and plodded to the kitchen to test her theory, leaving Tyler to sleep for a little while longer. It was, after all, Saturday.

Soon Hope had bacon and eggs for two cooking on the stove, waiting for the urge to heave to kick in.

Still nothing, much to her delight. It seemed as if her morning sickness had simply disappeared overnight. Had her body been on a countdown, just waiting to shift into the second trimester?

Thank You, Jesus. What would she have done if she'd gone on to have one of those pregnancies plagued with the unpleasant symptom for the entire nine months? Then again, she might just be having a good day. But after weeks of the morning bathroom sprint the moment she awoke, Hope suspected she'd rounded the corner.

And now, finally, they could tell their family and friends.

Hearing footsteps, she glanced over her shoulder.

Tyler stumbled into the kitchen, stretching out his back and yawning. He raked his fingers through his ruffled hair. She loved how cute he looked first thing in the morning, like a little boy in nothing more than his long, gray and white striped pajama pants.

"*Ku'uipo*, what are you doing up? I specially left you to sleep in." Hope eased the spatula beneath one egg, loosening it from the pan.

"I thought I smelled breakfast cooking. Mmm, haven't had that aroma wafting through our home in... Well, since you got pregnant." Tyler wrapped his arms around Hope, giving her tummy a gentle rub. "I just love this little baby-belly pooch."

He kissed Hope in the neck, and she giggled. "That tickles."

She turned to him, grinning. "I think my morning sickness has finally disappeared. *And* my appetite has returned."

"I'm so glad, honey. And not only because we can now enjoy our favorite breakfast. I hated seeing you start each day feeling so ill."

"And I'm tired of living on crackers and ginger tea first thing in the morning." Hope set out two plates then popped a slice of toast onto each before dishing up the bacon and eggs. She shifted the plates to the end of the breakfast counter. "Crazy to think how tired and sick our little Gen Z has made me, and he or she is barely the size of a lemon."

Already diving into his bacon and eggs as if it were the first time he'd eaten them, Tyler grunted a response. It wasn't hard to tell he'd been deprived for weeks. He closed his eyes, lifted his face to the ceiling, and moaned. "This is soooo good."

"I'm happy you like it." Hope tittered. "I was a little worried I'd forgotten how to cook breakfast."

Frowning, she sat down. "Don't you think we should bless the food first? Especially as I'm a little rusty in the breakfast department."

Tyler shut his eyes and rattled off a quick prayer.

Elbow to the table, he rested his chin in his palm and stared at Hope. A twinkle glinted in his eye. "So today's the day we can tell everyone?"

Hope nodded. She was just as eager to let everyone in on their secret, but food had seemed way more important this morning. "Soon as we're done here."

Tyler shook his head. "Um, not quite. It's only two a.m. in Hawaii, six a.m. in Colorado, and seven a.m. in Kansas."

"Ha, true. I didn't think about the time zone differences." Hope prodded her temple. "Baby mush up there at the moment."

"Don't be so hard on yourself, honey—it's all those extra hormones, that's all. Why don't we have another look on the internet at what houses are listed this week? Maybe we can try to set up some viewings for this afternoon. Once we're back home, we can call our families."

Pensive, Tyler drove his SUV in the direction of the Clearwater Country Club, following close behind the real-estate agent's vehicle. *Please, Lord, let this be the home for us.* Despite the previous two listings that looked promising on the internet, there were many features on each that Hope had just not liked. He could've worked around some of the issues, but Hope was adamant they just weren't the house she envisaged raising their children in.

He glanced at Hope and offered a hesitant smile. "Maybe it'll be third time lucky, honey?"

She crossed her arms and blew out a huff. "Third for today. But what about all the other houses we've looked at over the past few weeks that haven't been right? Am I setting my standards too high, *ku'uipo*? Is there such a thing as the perfect home?"

Tyler reached for her leg and squeezed, the cotton of her loose-fitting pants soft to his touch. "Of course there is. We'll know it when we see it. We still have ample time."

"Which is running out fast! I'm almost four months pregnant. We need to be in our new home by the time I'm seven months, so really, that only leaves us with a month or two to find *and* buy a home. And who knows how long all that legal paperwork will take."

"Sometimes it can go fast." Most times probably not. At least not as fast as they'd like. "We could always buy after the baby is born."

Hope released a heavy sigh. "I know. But I so wanted to decorate a nursery for our firstborn. And that won't be possible in a one-bedroomed apartment."

"Have faith, honey. God has just the right home prepared for us. I've heard from many people that He's the best real estate agent around. And maybe this next house is it. I do have a good feeling."

They turned right onto a curved driveway and stopped beneath the thick, leafy boughs of a large willow oak. Its branches filled the length and breadth of the front yard.

"Ooh, I *love* this tree." Excitement raised Hope's pitch.

Tyler gazed past Hope through the passenger window, first at the enormous tree, allowing his eyes to roam further to the olive-green, two-story colonial-style house. Could this be their future home? Their dream house?

"So do I," he said. "We could build an incredible tree house up there if we have a boy."

Hope flashed a grin. "Or a dollhouse on the ground beneath if it's a girl."

"Then again, we might have a daughter who loves climbing trees." Tyler chuckled as he clambered out of the car and hurried around to the passenger side to help Hope out.

"What year did you say this house was built?" he asked Margaret, the middle-aged real-estate agent, as she approached.

Margaret turned to survey the listing. "This gorgeous home was built in 1923. Truly an incredibly rare find in a land full of modern single-story houses."

Tyler blew out a soft whistle. "Wow, that's a whole lot of living that's happened under that roof."

"I love the idea that the home has history." Hope smiled and took Tyler's hand.

"Shall we take a look inside?" Margaret led the way up the paved path to the front door.

Under the portico, Hope kicked off her sandals. Shoes were dirty and needed to be left outside she believed. She'd tried hard over the past two years to train Tyler to do the same. For the most part, he remembered, and soon knew all about it if he happened to forget.

Hope opened her mouth then shut it again as Margaret waltzed inside the grand foyer, still wearing her heels. Thankfully, they were wedges, because had they been stilettoes, they would surely have damaged the highly-glossed southern yellow pine floor.

The enormous living room on the left with its large windows on either side and lemon-colored walls was bright and airy. Opposite the front door, a staircase led up to the second floor, the steps clad in the same wood as the downstairs' floors. They strolled through the living room.

"What a gorgeous fireplace." Hope trailed her fingers across the breadth of the mantle. "I love it."

Tyler chuckled. "Not that we need one in our Sunshine State, but I guess there's still the *very* odd invasion of cooler air."

They stepped from the living room into the bright family room, windows filling the walls from one side of the room to the other.

"This will be the kids' playroom," Hope announced as she pirouetted across the floor.

"Kids?" Tyler called after her. "So how many *are* we going to have?"

Coming to a stop, she leaned against the windowsill and smiled. "As many as this house will take."

"You're pregnant?" Margaret's mouth curved upward.

Tyler shot Hope an anxious look. How should they respond? They hadn't told their families yet. Was a stranger to be the first to know?

Hope pursed her lips, widened her eyes, and shrugged.

Margaret chuckled. "I'd wondered if that was a baby bump. Congratulations. And this—" She circled, arm outstretched. "This is the perfect family home. Do you like what you see so far?"

"Like? Oh gosh, I *love* what I see." Hope scampered into the formal dining room, Tyler hot on her heels.

"Love it!" she squealed before dashing into the kitchen. "Oh yes! We can definitely feed a couple of kids in *this* kitchen. And those blue, brick-shaped wall tiles against the wooden cupboards... To die for."

Hope was like a kid in a candy store.

She swept her palms over the center island and the glass top stove. "Bacon and eggs, *ku'uipo*?"

On the other side of the island, Tyler squatted lower, pretending to seat himself on an imaginary stool. "Thank you. Two eggs, sunny-side up. And don't forget the toast and honey, honey."

Unable to keep the pose for too long, he straightened and surveyed the kitchen. "This has definitely had a recent revamp."

"Probably a few since 1923." Margaret ambled into the kitchen.

"The entire house has definitely had several modifications since it was built. There are many features that would not have been standard on the original build."

"Then I'm thankful I wasn't around in 1923 to buy this home." As Hope walked over to Tyler, she asked Margaret, "Can we go upstairs?"

Margaret smiled. "Of course. Feel free to roam wherever you want. And to ask anything you want." Her phone rang and she reached inside her bag for it. "I'm sorry, I need to take this. You go on ahead, I'll catch up. Oh, and there's a bedroom and bathroom downstairs. You might want to check that out first."

Down the passage, Tyler and Hope found the large bedroom with a walk-in closet and *en suite* bathroom. Likely some of those modifications Margaret had spoken of.

"For family, when they come to visit," he suggested.

Hope strode across to the window and squealed. "Look at the screened pool outside!"

Tyler came to stand beside her. He fist pumped the air. "Yes! That glass covering will keep the water cleaner. Not to mention keeping out unwanted visitors."

"Like our little munchkins?" She literally glowed and Tyler was no longer sure whether it was because of the pregnancy or delight at this house.

He shook his head and pinched Hope's cheek. "No... Like snakes and birds and frogs."

She screwed up her face. "Ew. Then I'm glad it's there. But, creepy crawlies aside, it is a great safety feature until our children have learned to swim."

"Which, knowing you, won't take too long. I think you'll have them swimming before they can crawl. Maybe before they can roll over."

"Knowing me, I will." She took Tyler's hand. "Come, let's see

20

what's upstairs."

Beneath the staircase was a small guest bathroom. Tyler peeked inside. "Now that is handy."

"And necessary," Hope added before flouncing up the stairs, her tiny baby-bump leading the way.

Tyler followed close behind her.

Just off the landing was a long, narrow room. Tyler glanced around. "This will make a perfect office."

"Or another playroom." Hope stared at him, one brow rising. "Besides, since when did either of us need a home office?"

"All right, you win. Guess with all the children we plan to fill this house with, one playroom will never do."

"Thank you, *ku'uipo*." Hope wrapped her arms around Tyler's neck and sighed. "I love this house so much, but can we afford it?"

"Well, it might be a little tight in the beginning, but there is talk of an imminent promotion for me to Head of Research and Development…"

Hope leaned back, searching Tyler's eyes. "What? That's wonderful news, *ko'u aloha*. Why didn't you tell me?"

"I didn't want to say anything until it was official. But now seemed like the right time to let you know."

Taking Hope's hand, Tyler led her down the passage into the main bedroom. Once again, they took in the view out the window. "We do need to get into the property market, and this will be a great investment. It's in a good neighborhood. And with that golf course across the road, I might just be tempted to take up the game."

Hope burst out laughing. "Right…like I can see you chasing a little white ball around. If golf were played in the ocean, then maybe, but out there under the hot sun with not a drop of water to cool you… I just can't see that happening."

"You're probably right, honey. But I'm sure Faith's hubby,

Charles, will want to drag me out for a game if they come to visit."

"*When* they come to visit. But we're getting ahead of ourselves. We haven't bought this house yet. There's still a big chance we might not be the lucky ones to secure it."

They continued on to examine the first bedroom closest to the master bedroom. A soft sea green covered the walls.

"This will be the nursery," Hope announced. "It's perfect."

"I like the fact that every room has a ceiling fan. A necessary feature as far as I'm concerned." Tyler opened the built-in closet to check out the storage space. Definitely a later addition, for a house this old would've been furnished with free-standing wardrobes. But he was more than glad they wouldn't have to have closets installed because that would cost more than a couple hundred dollars.

They checked out the third upstairs bedroom.

Just as they stepped into the bathroom, Margaret caught up with them. "So, what do you think?"

Tyler and Hope whirled around to face the agent.

"I love the 'his and hers' basins," Hope said, "but this flowery wallpaper will have to go. As will some of the brighter colors in a few of the rooms." She chuckled. "They hurt my eyes."

Tyler's gaze skirted the bathroom walls, coming to rest on Hope. "Finishing touches, honey. Easy enough to fix. And at least the nursery and our bedroom won't need a repaint."

Hope slid her arm around Tyler's. She beamed with delight. "I love this house. Well, ninety-nine percent of it. And best of all, it's not far from either of our jobs or the beach."

"It is a wonderful home." Margaret's smile skewed to one side. "However, I have some bad news. The people I showed the property to this morning want to make an offer. That was them on the line. But I'd so love for you to have this house, what with a family on the way. This is the perfect home to raise children."

She raised a cautious hand, shaking her head. "I don't want to rush you into a decision. However, if you *are* interested, I'd encourage you to get an offer in fast."

CHAPTER FOUR

ALMOST TOUCHING the horizon, the sun set the ocean and sky on fire in a blaze of orange. Despite Hope's chatter, Tyler remained withdrawn as he drove home, the house issue clearly on his mind.

She eyed him, hesitant to broach the subject this soon. But time wasn't on their side, and if they didn't make a quick decision—something Tyler hated doing—they could lose this house. One good thing was that he had seemed keen on the property. But was that enough to get him to make a decision today? However, if he didn't decide by tomorrow's deadline, she might just have to throw a temper tantrum and blame it on her raging hormones later.

Hope drew in a deep breath. It was now or never. Well maybe not never…that was a bit dramatic. She rested a hand on Tyler's shoulder, her finger softly caressing his neck. She'd try the gentle approach first. It usually worked. "*Ku'uipo*, what are we going to do about that house?"

Tyler released a heavy sigh, and a knot formed in Hope's belly. She didn't want to go to DEFCON 1, but she would if she had to. Drastic times called for drastic measures, and war would be imminent should Tyler drag his feet on this decision.

"I'd never given it a thought that we could find ourselves in a situation where we'd be forced to make a hasty choice, but I guess we just have to." He glanced at her before returning his attention to the road. "When we get home, let's pray about it, then give it some time for God to speak. Maybe we'll get clarity after chatting to our families about the baby."

It wasn't the immediate yes she'd hoped for, but at least it wasn't a no. What was it that he could never just say yes without having to churn something over, and over, and over?

She pushed her exasperation aside and managed a smile. "Sounds like a plan. But remember, we only have until tomorrow morning to call Margaret."

Once they were back inside their apartment, they headed for the living room and sank to their knees beside the couch. After spending some time in prayer, they shifted to sit on the soft cushions and Tyler dialed her parents' number, insisting it was only fair they should hear before his siblings.

Hope took the phone from him just as the landline was answered on the other side.

"*Aloha.*" Her mother's voice drifted through the earpiece.

Emotion tightened Hope's throat. She sucked in a breath. "*Makuahine…*"

"Nakine… What is it *keiki*? Is everything all right?"

Mother always called her Nakine, the Hawaiian version of her name. Would her mom still refer to her as a child when she found out Hope was about to become a mother herself?

Hope nodded. "Everything is just wonderful, *Makuahine.* I'm calling to tell you that I'm pregnant...*hāpai.*"

"That is wonderful news. *Akua,* is good."

"He is, Mom. All the time."

"Peni," Mother called to Father, "Nakine is *hāpai!*"

Mother was so excited, one would think this was her first grandchild, but with Hope being the only girl and the youngest of their six children, this was probably very special news for her parents. Especially her mom.

Father's chuckles and good wishes drifted faintly through the phone. He was probably sitting in his favorite chair in the adjoining living room.

"I guess you will have to find a house now," her mother said. "A nice green one to remind you of the mountains of Hawaii, *'ae*?"

Hope's heart thumped against her chest. Yes! Definitely. A green one like they'd seen today. Actually, it was the only green house they'd seen, period. Was her mother's strange suggestion perhaps God giving them the go-ahead? A *green* light? She couldn't wait to see what Tyler thought.

After chatting with her mother about the pregnancy—how far along she was, her daily morning sickness and when the baby was due—she handed the phone to Tyler.

He had a quick word with her mom then cut the call.

"Your turn," Hope told him. "Who are you going to call first?"

Tyler frowned. "Don't you want to contact your brothers next?"

She shook her head. "Mom will take care of that."

"All right, if you're sure. I'll call Faith first, then I'll contact Brody."

"You're close to your sister, aren't you?"

Tyler cracked a grin. "Guilty as charged. There's almost a decade between me and my brother. Faith a little less at seven years. But despite the large age gaps, she's always been there for me."

"We need to visit them in Colorado sometime. Or have Faith and her family visit here. I fear I haven't spent nearly enough time getting to know her. But in my defense, we've only been married a year, and it's been a busy one settling into a new environment and job. Plus, we do all live in different States."

"Well, Colorado wasn't on the cards for us, even though it's home to me. There's no ocean, only mountains."

Tyler stretched his arm around the back of the couch and pulled Hope closer. He tapped his finger to her nose. "There'll be no traveling for you for a while, so we will just have to invite them to visit. Maybe once we're settled in our new home…"

Hope's eyes widened. "Does that mean you've come to a decision?"

Shaking his head, Tyler grinned. "Not quite, honey. We have only just prayed about it, so still waiting for God to give us a sign that the green house is the one for us."

Hope shifted in her seat. Elbow digging into the top of the couch, she rested her chin on her fist, her gaze searching his. "Well then, I should tell you what my mother just said."

CHAPTER FIVE

THE SUNDAY morning service had been amazing—wonderful worship, powerful preaching, and passionate prayers. Recharged and renewed, Hope felt so close to God.

Standing on her own in the court of fellowship, Hope sipped her tea. Tyler had swigged down a cup of coffee and then "quickly" gone to make final arrangements with some of the youth to help out with their upcoming move on Saturday. She knew her husband's "quickly", especially when he got around the younger men of the church who were always eager to probe his brilliant mind. And what teenage boy living in Clearwater wouldn't be interested in marine robots and exploring the depths of the ocean? Besides, with her out of action to do any lifting or heavy work— Tyler's orders—they needed those young men's muscle power.

She took another mouthful of the hot liquid. Who would've thought that in a mere three weeks they'd bought a house and were preparing to move? Seemed unreal to think they'd be spending Christmas in their new home in less than a month.

"Yoo-hoo, Hope. *Aloha…*" Diana Martin, the lead singer in the worship team waved and hurried toward her. Diana was a bubbly young mother of twin toddlers. Or was that terrorists? Hope was glad Diana's little boys were nowhere to be seen. Her hubby must be watching them—or perhaps they were still running circles around their poor Sunday school teacher.

Diana flashed Hope a wide grin. "I'm so glad I managed to catch you today. I was watching you from the stage during worship and wanted to tell you that pregnancy suits you. You're positively glowing, girl."

She rubbed a hand across Hope's tummy. "Just look at this little baby-bump. I love it! Makes me yearn for another."

Hope giggled. Heaven help them all if the Martins had another child like the other two.

"Do you mind if I pray for your baby?" Diana asked.

Mind? She'd appreciate it. She'd been a little concerned when week sixteen passed with no sign of life. Now she was embarking on week seventeen with still no flutters in her belly except for her nerves. Even though those first signs could appear anywhere between week sixteen and week twenty-five she'd read. Still, to be on the safe side, she'd make an appointment this week to see her doctor.

Hope offered Diana a wide smile. "I would love it if you prayed for my baby."

"Wonderful. Shall we move to the cry room? It's a little more private and should be empty by now."

"Great idea." Hope swallowed the last of her tea then tossed the Styrofoam cup in the trash.

She followed Diana into the back of the church, and they slipped inside the small room with its one-way glass looking into the sanctuary. Empty. Only the faintest odor of a throwaway diaper remained, trapped between the walls. Hope shot a prayer of thanks heavenward that her morning sickness had been a thing of the past for twenty-two days and counting. Without a doubt, a few weeks ago that whiff would've sent her dashing for the ladies room.

Diana fanned the air in front of her nose then chuckled. "Whew, some mommy had a humdinger to clean. I've certainly had my fair share of them. Ha, maybe it was even one of my boys. Thankfully, if it was, that would've been hubby's job to take care of once he'd fetched them from the toddlers' class."

Hope eyed the empty trash can. "And thankfully, whoever it was, had the sense to take that stinky diaper home with them, or we wouldn't have been able to pray in here."

"You're so right, although the church doesn't expect parents to do that. I mean, I wouldn't want to carry a smelly diaper home. Someone cleans up after the services, including the cry room, so perhaps they've already been."

Diana sank into a chair, gesturing for Hope to take the one next to her. "Are you ready for everything that motherhood is going to throw at you?"

Hope nodded then skewed her mouth. "Just not sure about the stinky diapers."

Diana leaned closer and whispered. "I'll let you in on a little secret—that's when you hand the baby over to Tyler."

"Looks as if I'm going to have to come to you for some tips and lessons."

"Anytime." Diana placed her hands on Hope's belly. "Should we pray?"

Before Hope could answer, Diana closed her eyes.

"Abba Father, giver of life, thank You for this precious baby You've blessed Hope and Tyler with. Lord, we stand amazed at how fearfully and wonderfully we are all made, and praise You that You are weaving this little baby together in Hope's womb. This child's frame isn't hidden from You—Your eyes see this unformed body. This infant's days are already written in Your book.

"Lord, You have a purpose for every breath this baby takes and every beat of its heart. You give each new life a hope and a future—this little one is no exception. May this life be for Your glory alone.

"Father, I pray for strength for Hope in this pregnancy. No matter what happens in the future, help her to rest in Your omniscience and surrender any fears or worries. Hope and Tyler will be amazing parents. May this child leap for joy at that blessing."

Beneath Diana's hands, Hope felt an unexpected flutter in her belly, like a tiny fish skittering through the amniotic fluid in her womb. Her breath hitched and her eyes flew open.

"Did you feel that?" she whispered.

Diana peered out of one eye before she opened the other. She shook her head. "Feel what?"

"L–like a butterfly, or a fish… Something strange…different."

Diana chuckled. "I take it you haven't felt the baby move yet?"

"No."

"Well, that was your baby making its movements known to you. Nobody, except you, will be able to feel it initially. This is your special moment. But in a few weeks, Tyler will be able to place his hand on your tummy and feel your baby's kicks too."

Hope grinned. "Oh, I can't wait. And I can't wait to tell Tyler that the baby moved. But I apologize—I interrupted your beautiful prayer. Please continue."

"Well, all I was still going to pray was—" Smiling, Diana closed her eyes again. "In Your amazing and powerful name we pray and ask these things. Amen."

Exhausted and ready for bed, Tyler strapped the last box closed then pushed it into the small living room and stacked it beside the other boxes filling one wall. Finally, they were ready for the big move tomorrow. And early next week, the extra furniture they'd had to buy would be delivered. He certainly looked forward to eating dinners at their new dining room table and not on the couch or at the kitchen counter.

Stepping back, he surveyed the room. Who would've thought they had so much stuff? Although, in the bigger house, it would probably all disappear into near oblivion, and they'd need to go out shopping for more things to fill their new home. Hope already had plans to get the nursery ready before the end of the year.

He ambled back into the bedroom. Hope had just stepped out of the shower. She slid her nightshirt over her head. The fabric hugged her belly.

"You won't be able to wear that for too much longer, honey."

She pouted and sank onto their bed. "I know. I'm getting so fat."

Leaning over, Tyler kissed her. "No you're not. You're just perfect." He placed his hands on either side of Hope. Towering above her, he eased her down onto the cool, linen covers beneath.

She giggled and pushed him away. "*You* need a shower before you're coming anywhere near me."

"That can be arranged. Fast." He whipped off his shirt and dashed into the bathroom.

The hot shower soothed his aching muscles. Refusing to allow Hope to do much, he'd had to work twice as hard. But it was worth it to avoid any harm coming to the baby.

He leaned against the tiled wall and closed his eyes as the water splattered his body. *Lord, I praise You for all You have given me. A beautiful, full of fun, loving wife, a wonderful new home and a promotion enabling us to afford that, and to top it all, a baby on the way. I don't deserve Your favor, but I thank You.* A contented smile curved his lips. He was so ridiculously happy and incredibly blessed.

Would you still praise Me and thank Me if any of that was taken from you?

The thought hit Tyler as if someone had turned the water to cold. He pushed away from the wall and turned the shower faucet in the opposite direction. The overhead stream trickled to a stop. Could he ever say like Job, "though He slay me, yet will I hope in Him"? He didn't have an answer, and prayed he'd never have to have one.

CHAPTER SIX

A WARMTH filled Tyler as he gazed across the table at his wife. Even though it was only the two of them, she'd made the most scrumptious Christmas Eve dinner. Hope had outdone herself with the roast turkey, mashed potatoes and gravy, and oven-browned root vegetables.

How he loved her—more and more with each passing day.

Sitting there with her little Santa hat on, Hope had such a beautiful glow about her that he could be tempted to keep her pregnant forever.

"Honey, that was delicious. I didn't think I could, but I ate it all. Every last morsel." He lifted his empty plate to show her.

Hope giggled. "I'm glad you enjoyed it, *ku'uipo*. I wanted tonight to be special. I was tempted to do a traditional Christmas *luau*, but the Hawaiian holiday dinner is so different, I wasn't sure you'd like it."

"Well, how about we spend next Christmas with your parents in Honolulu and I can find out for myself?"

Hope's mouth stretched into a wide smile. "I'd like that very much."

She dabbed her lips with her napkin then folded the small, square cloth and set it down beside her plate. "Why don't we relax beside the Christmas tree, maybe sing a few carols? I'll serve dessert a little later with coffee. Or hot chocolate."

"An excellent idea, my love." Tyler pushed to his feet. "So, what's for dessert?"

Hope slowly rose from her chair as well. She grinned. "Plum pudding."

"Plum pudding? Oh yum!" He ran his tongue between his lips. "My favorite. My mom always made it at Christmastime."

"I know." Hope's eyes held a twinkle.

"You do? How?" He couldn't remember telling her, but he must have.

A laugh bubbled from her mouth. "I called Faith. She told me a lot of things about you, *ku'uipo*."

Tyler gulped. "Good things, I hope."

"Mostly."

Shaking his head, Tyler leaned across the table and grabbed Hope's almost empty plate. He set it down on top of his. "Run along to the living room, honey. I'll clear up here and stack the dishwasher. It'll only take a few minutes. The last thing we want to wake up to on Christmas Day is a dirty dining room and kitchen."

Hope grabbed the glasses from the table. "I'll help."

Tyler rushed to her side of the table. He set the plates down then eased the glasses out of Hope's hands. Fingers clutching the glassware, he pointed toward the living room. "Go. Relax. I've got this. You've done enough for today making this amazing meal."

"All right." Her dark hair swayed from side to side as she hurried from their formal dining room, the pom-pom at the end of her hat dancing behind her.

After Tyler had filled the dishwasher and wiped down the counters, he headed for the living room.

Hope sat on the rug in front of the large Christmas tree with its twinkling lights, legs outstretched, tummy filling the space in front of her. The aroma of cinnamon wafted through the room.

"Hmm, something smells good in here."

Looking up, Hope flashed him a grin. "Cinnamon-scented candles. I bought them last week."

"Nice." He glanced at the empty hearth. If only the weather was cooler, they could have used the fireplace.

Tyler grabbed his guitar from the corner of the room then sat down on the couch close to Hope. "Smells just like Christmas. All we need now is a cold snap so we can light that fire. And maybe a few light flurries of snow falling outside."

She gazed up at him. "Like that will happen. We'll just have to do a Christmas in Colorado. Year after next?"

"Sure, why not?" At this rate, they'd have all their Christmases planned until their son or daughter left for college.

Resting the guitar on his thigh, he strummed the first chords for "Silent Night".

Hope hummed along for a verse before she began to sing. Her angelic voice echoed through the room. Finally, it really felt like Christmas.

After singing several carols together, Tyler set his guitar down on the floor and patted the cushion beside him.

Hope crawled onto the couch and snuggled up against him. She released a contented sigh before turning her head to gaze at Tyler. "Can you believe we're past the halfway mark? Seven more weeks and we'll be in the third trimester…the home stretch."

Tyler tightened his embrace. "I can't wait to meet our little Gen Z."

"Me too." Her mouth curved like a crescent moon. "You ready for that plum pudding yet?"

"In a little while." He was still quite stuffed from dinner.

Perhaps they should've gone caroling in the neighborhood to walk off their meal. But it had been so special sitting there beside the tree, just him and Hope, and baby bump, who still wasn't letting his or her presence be known to anyone except Mommy.

Tyler leaned forward and kissed Hope on the lips. Long and passionately. Finally, he drew away and relaxed back into the couch.

Wrapping an arm around him, Hope rested her head on his chest. "I could lie here and do that forever."

"Me too." Placing a finger beneath her chin, Tyler tipped Hope's head up and went in for another of those delicious kisses. Who needed plum pudding when they had such succulence to feast upon?

When Tyler's mouth released Hope's lips, he smoothed a hand over her belly. "So, have you thought of any more baby names for our little one? Besides Gen Z."

"Hmm, I have a few in mind. If it's a girl, what about Mae?"

He frowned. "Mae? A family name I'm not aware of?"

Hope maneuvered herself into an upright position. "No. Because she's due in May."

Brows quirking upward, Tyler exclaimed, "You're joking, aren't you?"

Hope burst into laughter. She slapped her palm against his stomach lightly. "Of course I'm joking."

Without warning, she sucked in a sharp breath. "Ooh, did you feel that? Either Gen Z loves that name or hates it."

Grabbing Tyler's hand, she placed it on the side of her tummy. This time he felt the movements and prods coming from within. Excitement, fear, and wonder filled him. The fact that Hope had their baby growing inside of her suddenly became very real.

With Christmas behind them, Hope and Tyler stood on the brink of a new year. Tonight they would see 2002 in at a midnight service. And then they could say, "This year, our baby will be born."

While Tyler checked that he'd tightened all the screws on the newly-assembled crib, Hope gazed around the nursery, a sense of satisfaction and accomplishment overwhelming her. If this little baby didn't grow up to be a lover of the sea as well, then she'd be gobsmacked. In fact, she'd stake her flippers and snorkel on him or her being a beach baby.

The sea green walls and white furnishings reminded Hope of the foamy whitecaps on the ocean. On the two walls surrounding the crib, they'd painted waves and attached fish and sea turtle stickers. The remaining wall was adorned with four block-mounted 3D pictures—an anchor and lifebuoy ring, seahorse and seaweed, starfish and shells, and a yacht with a breaker lapping its bow.

The green and white linen in the crib looked so fresh and the armchair for nursing so comfy. A beige rug covered the wooden floor in the center of the nursery, mimicking beach sand. Oh, their baby was going to sleep well in this room. And she would spend many, many happy hours bathing, clothing, and feeding their little one here.

Hope finished hanging the toy seahorses and starfish on the baby mobile and passed it to Tyler. "Thank you for helping me to finish the nursery before the year's end."

About to attach the mobile to the top end of the crib, Tyler paused. He glanced up at Hope. "You set a deadline for when you wanted it done, although we only just made it with a few hours to spare. It's been such fun working on this at night with you, honey. You've done an amazing job with the décor, as you always do."

She had. Even if she had to say so herself. Which she didn't because Tyler had just said so.

She released a lengthy sigh.

"And that sigh?" Tyler asked, fastening the mobile.

Hope lifted one shoulder in a shrug. She inhaled deeply then exhaled. "Do you realize that none of our family will get to see me pregnant, except for photos, of course? And even though it was so awesome spending Christmas with only you, I do wish we could've had some family this year."

Tyler stepped closer to Hope and wrapped her in his embrace. He smoothed a finger over her cheek as he gazed deep into her eyes. "Oh, honey, me too. But it just wasn't possible with the move being so close to Christmas. It took us all that time just to get the house straightened. Think how difficult it would've been if we'd still needed to entertain guests. Besides, we don't even have beds or bedding yet for the extra rooms."

"True." They'd spent so much getting the nursery, dining room, and living room looking good, they'd have to save for a few more months before they could tackle the two spare bedrooms. All they'd done for now was to hang curtains. Then they'd closed the doors on the empty spaces. If anyone made any surprise visits though, they'd have to rush out and buy the beds and linen—break the bank and be done with it.

CHAPTER SEVEN

HOPE ROLLED out of bed. She would have bounced from the mattress to the floor had her stomach not started to become just a teensy bit cumbersome these days. What was she going to be like when she got to nine months? A beached whale?

Giving a contented stretch, she arched her back and reached toward the ceiling. Today was going to be awesome. Ethan had called earlier to tell her he was headed for Tampa Bay. At dawn, a pregnant bottlenose dolphin had been found in distress in shallow waters near Pass-a-Grille Channel, struggling to give birth. It seemed the calf was stuck. If the mother didn't get help, both she and her pup would die. Time was ticking, but the rescue team would need to bring her to the medical tank at the center—it would be far too difficult to help a wild dolphin in trouble deliver out in the ocean.

Hope decided to go in to work a little later as it would take a while before Ethan and the rescue team arrived back at the aquarium. She was glad—not about the dolphin, although she was excited that she got to do what she loved and that was help hurting sea creatures—but rather because she could smell the faint aroma of bacon and eggs frying downstairs. At least now she could enjoy this meal at a more leisurely pace. It could be a long and taxing day ahead, and she'd need all the sustenance she could get. Especially as she was feeding two.

Gazing across the room, Hope paused to once again appreciate the huge bunch of fresh, red roses standing in a vase on her dresser. Wow! Tyler certainly was pulling out all the stops this Valentine's Day. Roses, breakfast, plus he'd made dinner reservations at their favorite steakhouse overlooking Clearwater Beach and the Gulf of Mexico. There was nothing quite as romantic as watching the sun setting over the ocean while dining by candlelight.

Inside her womb the baby moved, contorting Hope's belly.

"Good morning, little one." She rubbed the side of her stomach, and the baby eased back on the stretch. Just into the third trimester, their baby, now the size of an eggplant and weighing just over two pounds, was perfectly formed and would have started to open and blink his or her eyes. That was according to her pregnancy books and Doctor Phillips whom she'd seen on Monday. Every two weeks from now on until her thirty-sixth week, she'd have appointments with the good doctor. Then it would be weekly visits until the baby was born.

"What do you see, little one?" she whispered as she reached inside her closet for her uniform. Thankfully she'd be going on maternity leave in another eight weeks, because her shirt could definitely not stretch too much further. She might even need to ditch the uniform earlier, or get a bigger shirt.

Once dressed in her knee-length lycra pants and branded royal blue T-shirt, Hope ambled downstairs with a little surprise of her own for Tyler. Hands behind her back, she waddled into the kitchen.

Tyler whirled around. "Hey, honey. What are you doing up? I

was going to bring you breakfast in bed."

"I wanted to enjoy it with you." She leaned in and kissed Tyler on the cheek. His morning bristles pricked her lips. "Happy Valentine's Day…again."

She peeked through the window. The sun shone gloriously outside. "Why don't I set the table beside the pool? We can eat out there."

"That's a great idea. Thanks. I'm almost done cooking." His gaze lowered to Hope's hands, hidden behind her back. "What are you up to?"

"I have something I wanted to show you." She whipped out the Doppler and tube of gel she'd been hiding.

"Y-e-s…" He dragged out the word, suspicion in his voice. "One of the tools of your trade, I know. You hinting for a new one?"

She giggled. "No. I borrowed this from work when I left yesterday, but I have to take it back today…before Ethan starts looking for it. I just wanted to treat you to something special this morning."

Tyler moved the pan with the eggs away from the hot plate and turned to her.

Hope squeezed a dab of gel onto the flat end of the probe. She switched on the small machine, then placed the probe against her belly, moving it around on one side, low down beneath her navel.

Suddenly the speaker came to life with a rapid swish, swish, swish.

Tyler's face lit up.

"I wanted you to hear the baby's heartbeat right here at home, *ku'uipo*."

Tyler tapped on the speaker. "Hey little one." His whisper was filled with wonder. He gazed up at Hope. "That is the best Valentine's Day gift you could have ever given me."

Hope grinned. "I thought you'd like it."

"I do." His smile morphed into a frown. "Do you really need to handle this dolphin birth today? I'm concerned."

She set the Doppler down on the kitchen counter then lightly cupped his cheek. "You worry too much, *ku'uipo*. I'll be fine."

En route to the rescue center, Hope received another call from Ethan. She tapped the Bluetooth receiver attached to her ear, a Christmas gift from Tyler.

"Ethan, talk to me. What's happening?"

"We're on our way. Be there in under thirty. I'm doing what I can for this distressed mamma, but I have to tell you, it's not looking good. I don't think this calf's alive. Should I give her a dose of Oxytocin?"

"No. A stillbirth is going to make assisting her that much harder. Last thing we want is to hasten the process while you're mobile. We'll help her to deliver manually when you're here." How she wished she could be out there, assisting with the rescue, but in her condition, that wasn't wise. She just needed to be patient and ready to administer the best care she could once the dolphin was in their tank.

"Ethan, have you covered her with wet towels?"

"Of course, Hope."

"And are you keeping her moist with repeated dowsing?"

Ethan released a chuckle. "Hope, I know you want to be here, but we know what we're doing. You'll get your turn to help soon."

Hope puffed out her cheeks, then slowly expelled the excess air. "I know. Sorry. Thanks for keeping me updated. I'll be waiting for you." She cut the call and shot a prayer to heaven for the slightest chance to deliver a healthy calf.

Once at the rescue center, she scurried about prepping for the delivery.

Sandy was right there alongside her, helping.

"Hope, I know I'm not medically trained, but if you need me to assist in any way during the delivery, just let me know."

Sandy was somewhat of a dolphin whisperer—her way with marine mammals could come in really handy in this case.

She glanced up at the pretty brunette. "Thanks. I'll definitely bear that in mind. Let's just see how many hands we have on deck when the team arrives."

Hearing the sound of the rescue vehicle pulling to a stop outside, Hope dashed toward the exit, eager to help.

"Hope, wait!" Sandy followed hot on her heels. "Let them get her into the tank, *then* you can get involved. You don't want to risk hurting your own baby, do you?"

She was right. Hope slowed her pace to a brisk walk. She turned to Sandy who'd managed to catch up to her. "All right, but I want to watch from the sidelines."

Sandy pointed a finger at her. "Sidelines... I'm going to have my eye on you, ready to blow the whistle if you move offside." She skewed her mouth. "Sorry, but it's for your own good."

When the dolphin was finally in the medical tank, and the water level had been reduced, Hope slid into the tank—as did Ethan, another two rescue team members, and at Hope's request, Sandy. Hope immediately began to assess the mammal.

As if sensing they were all there to help, the dolphin rolled over, baring her belly and the tiny flukes extending from her smooth underside. One look and Hope knew that the birth process had not progressed since the call had come in nearly five hours ago. Same amount of tail showing as in the photographs she'd received from Ethan.

She gripped either side of the tiny tail and tugged. The calf was really stuck. No way was she getting it out on her own.

Neither was the mother.

She glanced up. "Ethan, give me a hand down here."

Ethan shifted from where he'd stood at the dolphin's head beside Sandy. He took his place next to Hope, his eyes eagerly awaiting her command.

"You grab the right fluke, I'll take the left," she instructed. "On three, pull as hard as you can."

Waist-deep in water, Hope braced herself, toes curled in her waterproof shoes as they gripped the bottom of the tank. She counted, "One… Two… Three."

The calf shifted a few inches. At least it was progress, albeit little.

The pregnant cow strained, her breathing synchronizing with her efforts to give birth. Squeaks and trills resonated in the enclosed area.

Hope did another countdown before she and Ethan once again tugged on the calf's flukes, shifting the unborn a little farther out of the birth canal.

The mother rolled over, and they both lost their grip on the small tail. She pressed her abdomen against the bottom of the tank and thrashed her tail, sending Hope and Ethan flying back into the water.

After swallowing a mouthful of water, Hope made a swift recovery and rushed forward, only the mother's discomfort and pain on her mind.

The large, gray flukes flailed once more, this time connecting Hope across the left side of her stomach with a powerful thwack, taking her breath away.

CHAPTER EIGHT

CAREFULLY CLUTCHING his cup of coffee, Tyler hurried out of the office kitchen and headed in the direction of his desk. He had so much work to get through today, so many looming deadlines, and he'd already been detained far too long by their senior buyer, Milly Porter.

The middle-aged, dark-complexioned Louisiana woman had asked way too many questions about Tyler's impending fatherhood, and she hadn't seemed prepared to let him leave until he'd satisfied her curiosity. Was the baby a boy or a girl? Did they have any names picked out? How far along was Hope now? How was the pregnancy going? When was her due date? Was Hope planning to give up work and be a stay-at-home mom?

Tyler had answered her probing questions the best he could. Finally, he'd had to excuse himself.

"Hey, Tyler!"

The shout was unexpected and Tyler jerked, sending a sploosh of hot brew over the side of the porcelain mug and onto the carpet below. Thankfully the spill shouldn't show in the dark pile.

Tyler paused and turned. "Greg… I wanted to stop by your desk later today to check on how you're settling in." Greg Evert, Tyler's first recruit since he'd been promoted to Head of Research and Development, was a brilliant design engineer and an absolute asset to the team, even though he'd been there barely two weeks.

Greg neared, chuckling. "And I was about to come to your office, if that's okay. I've picked up some design flaws in our new model AUV that I need to discuss with you."

Tyler groaned inwardly. This latest autonomous underwater vehicle was giving him way more headaches than he cared for. He extended his hand, indicating that Greg should follow him to his office.

"So how's your wife? Not that long until you become a dad." Greg waggled his brows.

Tyler grinned. Talk of his wife and baby never failed to bring a smile to his face and warmth to his heart. "Only twelve more weeks. I can't believe it."

"It's quite an adjustment. Take my word."

Tyler clicked his fingers then pointed at Greg. "That's right. You became a father recently, didn't you?" He set his coffee cup down on his desk and sank into his chair.

Greg sat down on the opposite side of the table, a smile stretched across his face. "Eight months ago. And the best eight months of my life. Children truly are a gift from heaven. Man, I love that little guy of mine."

Tyler shook his head slowly and exhaled. "Yeah, I can't wait to meet our little one. And thanks, now you've made me even more eager."

"Ha, do not wish away your last few weeks of getting a good night's sleep. Your baby will be here soon enough, and then your life will change forever. But in a good way, I promise." Leaning forward, Greg rested his folded arms on the wooden desk. "Your wife still working?"

Tyler offered a nod. "I think if she had her way, she'd just transition from working, to giving birth, to going back to work without anyone noticing there'd been any change. Hey, if she had her way, I'm certain she'd opt for a water birth at the aquarium. Today she's helping a pregnant dolphin, rescued from the wild this morning, to give birth."

"Wow! That's exciting."

It sure was. Tyler hoped and prayed that it would be safe too. He hadn't been keen for Hope to take this case, but she was adamant. Sometimes his wife could be so stubborn.

"Hope!" Ethan lunged for Hope. His arms wrapped around her, dragging her out of the way of a second hit from the dolphin's tail. He shouted, "Sandy, do something to calm the beast!"

Hope spluttered, having swallowed water down the wrong pipe when she'd gasped and fallen at the fluke's impact. It had all happened so fast and unexpectedly. She wiggled out of Ethan's grasp. Nobody was taking away her right to help the birthing mom. She held up her palms to Ethan. "I'm fine."

Finding her footing, Hope shifted her attention back to the female dolphin as an orangey cloud suddenly appeared where she and Ethan had stood only moments before. A dark gray shadow dropped to the bottom of the tank.

Her heart squeezed with emotion and tears welled in her eyes. She swiped at them and turned to Ethan. "She's given birth. Thank you, Lord."

But the calf at the bottom of the pool remained motionless.

The mother calmed, and Hope wasn't sure if it was Sandy working her magic as she leaned in and stroked the dolphin's head, whispering to her, or utter relief at being out of the pain of giving birth, or purely a quiet resignation and acceptance that her pup was gone and nothing would bring it back. Knowing the creatures as she did, Hope was certain the cetacean's time of grieving would come. Even though the process of mourning had not yet been scientifically proven in dolphins, Hope had seen them display behavior that suggested they did lament.

How does a mother work through the loss of one that has been a part of your body for months?

Ethan stooped down, lifted the stillborn calf from the water, and cut the umbilical cord. The two slits on the calf's underside resembling an exclamation point instantly revealed its gender.

A male.

Hope gave the pup a once-over before instructing one of the rescue workers to take it inside to the OR. Later they'd carry out an autopsy on the body to determine a reason for the calf's death. Then she and Ethan went to work manually retrieving the rest of the placenta from the mother.

By the time Hope stepped out of the medical tank, she didn't feel well. The stress of the birth…the dead pup… It had all drained her emotionally.

Drying herself with a towel, she turned to Ethan. "Good job in there."

He smiled. "Thanks."

Stepping closer, he lightly grasped her arm. "Hey, are you okay? That was quite a blow you took out there."

"I'm fine. I already told you. But I am rather exhausted. Third trimester's taking its toll on me. Would you mind finishing up here? Give the mother three grams of Penicillin and Amoxycillin twice a day starting now, then release her into a tank on her own."

Hope turned to go, then paused. "Oh, and do you think you can handle the autopsy?"

"Do I—?" Excitement pitched his voice. "Of course, I can. Thanks, Hope."

She narrowed her gaze. "For what?"

"Trusting me with the responsibility."

She nodded. Truth was, on any other day, she wouldn't have entrusted these tasks to Ethan. When it came to work, she was a bit of a control freak. Okay, a lot of a control freak. But right now, she had to get out of there.

"I'll see you tomorrow." Hope shifted her gaze from Ethan to the top of the tank. She waved at Sandy. "Thanks for your help. You really calmed her when we needed it most."

Turning to the rest of the team still standing around, she bade them goodbye. "Remember team, we might've lost one today, but we definitely saved another."

She hurried away, fleeing for her Jeep.

Once back home, Hope showered then slipped into her robe and stretched out on top of her bed. She smoothed a hand over her stomach, a pink welt on the left side tattling about her encounter with the dolphin's tail.

"Hey little one," she whispered.

The baby remained silent. If she'd still had the Doppler at home, she would've used it, just to be sure all was well. But, her poor little baby was probably just as exhausted as she was from all the commotion today. She should've taken it easier. Nothing that a power nap couldn't sort out, though. And tonight, she'd dine with the love of her life, gazing at what she loved almost as much—the ocean.

Focusing on the vase of red roses, Hope soon drifted off to sleep.

Later, she woke to a searing pain in her stomach. How long had she been asleep? She curled into a ball. Something was very wrong. A stickiness clung to her inner thighs. She shifted and looked down, horrified. Red stained her legs, her robe, and the bed linen.

Hands trembling, she fumbled for her phone on the pedestal and dialed three digits.

The call was answered within seconds. "911, what's your emergency?"

CHAPTER NINE

SIRENS WAILED in the background as Tyler listened to the voice of the stranger. The air whooshed from his lungs as if someone had hit him hard in the gut. His legs threatened to collapse under him.

"W–what?" He could barely utter the single word.

"Your wife is bleeding, Mr. Peterson," the EMT repeated. "We're taking her to Labor and Delivery at Morton Plant Hospital."

"L–labor?" Could the baby survive at twenty-eight weeks?

"Yes."

"D–does Doctor Phillips, her obstetrician know?"

"The hospital will notify him."

"I'm on my way." A sudden burst of adrenalin had Tyler halfway to the elevator when he cut the call. The doors didn't open at the first press of the down button, so Tyler fled to the stairwell, taking the steps two at a time. It was only a couple of floors between his office and the basement parking.

He knew the road to the hospital well, having accompanied Hope to a few appointments at Doctor Phillips's consulting rooms nearby. Some he'd unfortunately had to miss due to work commitments. He should have put Hope first and gone with her to every one of them.

As his SUV sped down South Myrtle Avenue, he dialed his sister's number from his hands-free kit.

The phone rang several times.

He thumped the steering wheel. "Come on, come on, pick up the phone."

As if hearing him, Faith answered. "Tyler, this is a nice surprise. But you can't be calling to wish me a happy Valentine's Day. I'm your sister. What's up?"

Annoyance bubbled like a volcano, ready to spew. How could she be so chirpy when his world was crashing down?

Tyler drew in a deep breath, but when he spoke, all that came out of his mouth was a loud sob. The dam of tears he'd been holding back burst and his vision blurred, causing him to slow the vehicle.

"Tyler, what is it? What's wrong?" Faith's voice filled with concern.

"P–please p–pray for H–Hope. The baby— Hope's bleeding. She's on her way to the hospital in an ambulance." He couldn't believe he was saying those words.

"Oh Tyler, no. I'm so sorry. I'm down on my knees already. Please, keep me posted on her condition."

"I–I will. I have to go. I'm near the hospital, and I see an ambulance up ahead. Must be Hope."

Tyler cut the call, flicked on his turn signal and swung the SUV into the hospital parking lot. Finding an empty spot, he parked and ran for the entrance. He and Hope hadn't done a hospital tour yet, so he queried at reception where to find Labor and Delivery.

As he entered L&D, a man in a white coat rushed past Tyler, then glanced over his shoulder. "Tyler."

Doctor Phillips. *Thank you, Lord.*

He beckoned Tyler to follow.

The EMTs were still moving Hope from the gurney onto a bed when Tyler and the doctor entered the private room.

Seeing Tyler, Hope began to cry. "*Ko'u aloha*...I–I'm so s–sorry."

He rushed to her side, taking the opportunity to comfort her, if only for a few seconds. Stroking his fingers over her hair, he soothed, "It's going to be all right, honey. The doctors will fix this. And Faith is praying." He should have called the church, gotten Hope on the prayer chain. He huffed out a sigh. It would have to wait for now.

"I'm sorry, Mr. Peterson, but could you wait on the other side of the room?" the nurse attending Hope asked and began attaching a fetal monitor to Hope's belly.

Tyler nodded and moved out of the way, placing himself where he could still keep eye contact with Hope. And the doctor.

The EMTs exited the room, Doctor Phillips stepped up to the bed, stretching latex gloves over his hands. "Right, young lady. What's going on here?"

Doe-eyed and teary, Hope glanced across the room at Tyler before looking back to her obstetrician. "I–I don't know. I wasn't feeling well at work, so I went home, took a shower, and went to lie down. I must've slept for an hour or so, m–maybe longer, before I woke to severe cramping. T–that's when I saw all the b–blood." She broke down in a flood of tears. "Doc–doctor Phillips, I'm s–scared. A–am I going to l–lose my baby?"

The silver-haired obstetrician shook his head. "We'll do everything we can to prevent that, Hope."

He glanced at the fetal heart monitor, concern creasing his brow.

Was the machine even working yet?

"Did you have a fall recently?" Doctor Phillips asked.

"N–no." She flashed another look at Tyler, the fear in her eyes turning to resignation.

Or was that a look of regret?

"T–there was an incident at work…today."

An incident?

Tyler's pulse beat faster. He knew she shouldn't have gone to the rescue center this morning. The dolphin they were helping wasn't one of the tame ones that had been at the aquarium for years. He should have been firmer with her.

"What happened?" Unable to stop the words from gushing out of his mouth, Tyler's tone was far too curt for the situation. Immediately he regretted saying anything.

Hope squeezed her eyes shut, and her lips quivered.

She took a long, deep breath and exhaled. "W–we were waist-deep in the water, trying to pull a stillborn calf from a female dolphin. Suddenly, she thrashed in the water, and I… I took a hard b–blow to the stomach from her t–tail." Tears trickled across Hope's temples.

Tyler wanted to rush to her side, but he couldn't. He had to let the doctor do his work.

Opening her eyes, Hope focused her attention on her doctor. "I–is that what hurt my b–baby?"

Doctor Phillips pursed his lips before answering. "I'm afraid it's very possible, Hope."

He squeezed gel onto a transducer probe and glided it across her protruding belly as he studied the sonogram.

Tyler waited for the heartbeat, the same swishing sounds they'd heard only a few hours before. But all he could hear was the pounding in his ears as his own heart raced.

The nurse's gaze shifted, avoiding eye contact with Tyler and Hope.

Doctor Phillips leaned over Hope slightly, touching the left side of her stomach. "Hmm, there's bruising forming here."

Without warning, Hope yanked her legs up, knees pointing toward the ceiling as she clutched her stomach. That's when Tyler noticed the blood-stained sheet beneath her for the first time. Fear chilled his veins. Could there be any hope for their child?

Doctor Phillips returned the probe to the side of the machine, then moved to the bottom of the bed. He lifted the sheet to examine Hope. After what felt like forever, he glanced up at the fetal monitor, then at the nurse and shook his head.

Covering Hope's legs again, he sucked in a deep breath then exhaled, the furrows on his forehead deepening. He indicated for Tyler to come closer.

Tyler rushed to the other side of the bed and took Hope's hand in his.

Doctor Phillips's cleared his throat, sadness clouding his eyes. "Hope... Tyler... There is no easy way for me to say this. I'm afraid the blow to Hope's abdomen has caused a severe placental abruption."

Hope's gaze oscillated between Tyler and her doctor. "W–what does that mean? Bedrest? I–I can do that. I promise."

Doctor Phillips shook his head slowly. "You've started to dilate, Hope. But I'm afraid there's no longer a heartbeat. I'm so sorry, but your baby is—"

"Noooo..." Hope's eyes widened in disbelief before her face contorted with grief. "Noooo..."

Gripping her hand tighter, Tyler sank to his knees, his worst fears confirmed. He buried his face in the sheets and wept.

"Nurse, do a lab draw for a crossmatch and order two units A-positive. Get them running stat—Mrs. Peterson has lost enough blood already. And set up an IV line of oxytocin to speed up the contractions."

Doctor Phillips was silent for a moment before speaking again, his voice lowered, filled with compassion. "Hope, I'm sorry, I know this is very difficult, but you will still need to deliver your baby."

CHAPTER TEN

LEAVING HOPE to sleep, Tyler rose and went to stand beside the window, as had become his ritual in the past nine days, and would likely be as long as they lived in this house. He stared out of the window. The sun had just risen, lighting the tips of the willow oak's leaves. Would he ever get to build a treehouse between the great tree's boughs?

Even though he felt empty inside, his heart still pained within his chest. His throat tightened and his eyes stung. Once again, tears escaped in a flood of abandon.

Early in the new year, he and Hope had decided to name their child after his late father—if it were a boy.

Daniel Tyler Peterson.

Instead, as they'd held their son's perfectly formed body, not quite fifteen inches from top to toe, they chose the name Matthias—one of the names on their shortlist—for it means "the gift of the Lord".

Reflecting, Tyler wondered at the wisdom of their choice. Was he really a gift if God cruelly snatched him back?

The verse quoted at their son's funeral three days ago drifted into his mind, but it felt as if little Matthias himself were whispering the words in his daddy's ear.

Naked I came from my mother's womb, and naked I will depart. The Lord gave and the Lord has taken away; may the name of the Lord be praised.

Tyler muffled a sob. *Forgive me, Lord. Who am I to question You?*

Tyler vowed to add those words to the headstone when they had it made.

MATTHIAS TYLER DANIEL PETERSON
BORN FEBRUARY 14TH 2002
DIED FEBRUARY 14TH 2002
Gift of the Lord
"The Lord gave and the Lord has taken away.
May the name of the Lord be praised."

Unable to gaze any longer at the tree his son would never climb, Tyler turned away and headed downstairs. After the bustle of family in the house the past week, the place was deathly silent. But the worst silence was the absence of a baby's cry.

Faith had flown to Clearwater from Colorado with her son Michael the morning after Hope's delivery. Charles stayed behind, apparently to look after things at home. Faith had immediately taken over preparations for a full house. She'd ordered beds and mattresses for the two spare rooms and had them delivered that same afternoon. How she'd managed to get that right, he still didn't know. She'd bought bedding for both rooms, then stocked the fridge with sufficient food to feed an army for a week. By the time Hope's parents arrived the following day, they had a bed to sleep in and a hot meal to eat.

Faith and Michael had shared the upstairs room next to the nursery, while Hope's parents had stayed in the guest suite downstairs. The day before the funeral, three of Hope's brothers had flown in from Hawaii. They'd insisted on staying at a nearby B&B. Yesterday, everyone had returned home. Now it was just him and Hope. And she didn't seem to be there either.

Hope had been discharged from the hospital merely two days after the delivery. Tyler wished they'd kept her there longer because there were so many challenges she'd had to face—some he had never thought of. Like when her milk came in. Hope was in so much pain, with no baby to suckle on her engorged breasts to empty them. The course of nature had only exacerbated her belief that God was either unfair or He was punishing her. Or both. Either way, she reiterated over and over that He had deserted her.

And she refused to be consoled by the scriptures.

By anyone.

Tyler himself was walking the tightrope of trusting God or turning his back on Him. Some days, trust won. Other days, Tyler failed miserably. But he tried his best to keep it all together—if both he and Hope fell apart, there'd be no chance they'd see the light at the end of this very dark tunnel.

While in the hospital, Hope had a session every day with Doctor Montrose, a woman psychiatrist. Doctor Phillips had explained to Tyler that this was a necessary process in Hope's healing. Because her progesterone levels had dropped quickly with the sudden birth, there was a good chance that Hope would suffer from post-partum depression. Worse still, it could easily turn into major depression. They had to do everything possible to prevent Hope from disappearing down that slippery slope.

Doctor Phillips had suggested Tyler also see the shrink because he'd suffered a tremendous loss too. Unable to start this past week—he'd had a funeral to plan—come Monday, both he and Hope would have regular weekly visits with Doctor Montrose. Although not keen to spill his guts to a stranger—and on top of that, a woman—still, he would do what was necessary to keep a level head in order to help his wife.

His sister had been a godsend, not only in keeping the house together, but by assisting him with the most difficult task he'd ever had to do—bury his child. Hope was just not able to cope with anything at the moment, let alone make decisions on her baby's funeral.

Suddenly realizing that he stood in the middle of the kitchen, oblivious to everything around him, Tyler brushed his thoughts aside, filled the coffee machine and switched it on.

Sinking into a chair beside the center island, he stared at the flowers on the counter beneath the window. He'd bought them yesterday to put on the grave that afternoon. It would be their first visit since the funeral.

Although a myriad of bouquets filled their foyer and living room, Tyler had especially chosen this mix of orange and yellow snapdragons and kangaroo paws. Pretty pink flowers were for little girls, but boys...well they loved dragons and kangaroos, and fiery oranges and yellows.

Didn't they?

"Hey, honey, wake up. I brought you some breakfast."

Hearing Tyler's voice, Hope surfaced from her sleep for a brief moment before turning over and burying her head in the pillow. She didn't want breakfast. She didn't want to wake up. She just wanted to stay in the darkness of slumber where she didn't have to remember, didn't have to feel this heartache, pain, and regret. Didn't have to face that tiny grave again today.

But even in her unconsciousness, the nightmare so often followed.

"I'm not hungry," she muttered.

Tyler's hand brushed lightly across her back before his fingers gently massaged her shoulder. "Please, honey, you have to keep your strength up. Not eating won't help you."

Hope ignored his pleas. Sooner or later he'd have to give up and go away. She didn't want to face food. She didn't want to face him. She didn't want to face her guilt...his blame. Oh, he didn't say it, but he felt it. He had to. She'd been stupid enough to get into that tank. Everyone knew it. She had put their baby in danger. And now he was dead. Little Matty was dead. And it was all her fault.

"Please...leave me alone," she whispered, shedding silent tears. "Please..."

For a moment Tyler remained still, his hand motionless on her back. And then he pulled away, the mattress lightcning as he stood. Moments later the door clicked shut.

For hours, Hope tossed and turned, losing herself in the spiraling blackness that dragged her deeper and deeper into its abyss. Maybe if she fell for long enough, she'd never wake up. She could be reunited with her little one.

But murderers didn't go to heaven.

They went straight to hell.

Was she there already?

Her eyes shot open, and she jolted upright. She threw back the covers, rose, then trudged out of the bedroom.

Inside the bathroom, her gaze roamed the wallpaper, souring her mood further. Maybe she and Tyler should rather have expended their energy on this room first, instead of a nursery they had no use for. Reaching up, she pried her index finger behind a small piece of wallpaper that had started to come loose. Soon she'd ripped a chunk of the floral covering from the wall. She tossed it to the floor before stepping to the basin.

Hope stared at the boxes of medicine that filled the once empty shelf. Painkillers, tranquilizers, sleeping tablets, SSRIs. Never one for popping pills, she now stared down what seemed like an arsenal of them—some she'd never thought she'd see herself taking. Ever. Like the selective serotonin reuptake inhibitors, purported to correct the imbalance of serotonin in her brain. Frankly, the medication made her feel worse, not better. Now she suffered with tremors. She had trouble sleeping, and that in turn fed the need for the sleeping tablets. Of course, her difficulty to get a peaceful night's rest could also be attributed to the trauma she'd gone through, but the SSRI's package insert cited sleep disorders as one of the side-effects.

Also, she constantly felt nauseous, which had her dwelling on how much she wished she could rewind the clock to the time of her morning sickness and start this pregnancy all over again. She'd do it all differently if she had the chance. She'd resign from her job the moment those two blue lines formed on the pregnancy test. And then she'd cocoon herself and protect her baby from any and all harm.

Hope pressed a pill out of the blister pack and popped it into her mouth. She turned on the tap, leaned forward and filled her mouth with water. She swallowed. If this medication still made her feel sick after another week or two, she was stopping it. She'd rather take her chances on facing her demons alone than continue to feel as awful as she did.

She repeated the process with the pain meds and tranquilizer before undressing and stepping into the shower.

The water was warm and comforting. If only she could stay there forever, water cascading down her body and face. Here, nobody could see her tears—they simply mingled with the rest of the falling droplets.

She lowered her gaze to the shower floor where dark pink water swirled around the drain, and let out a low moan. Just one more unpleasant issue to deal with. How much longer would she bleed this heavily?

A knock sounded at the bathroom door. "Hope, honey, a–are you all right?"

I'll never be all right, is what she wanted to say. Instead she offered a soft, "Yes."

"Soon as you're showered and dressed, we can go to the cemetery, okay? I bought flowers yesterday for us to put on the grave."

She choked back a sob, managing an "Uh-huh" for Tyler's sake. Best she didn't keep him waiting too long. He'd been so patient with her already.

Placing her thumb above her left nipple and the first two fingers of her hand below it, Hope pressed back into the breast tissue to express some milk. Opaque liquid squirted from her milk ducts. Just enough to be comfortable once again had become her mantra.

Those first few days after her milk came in were so painful, not to mention devastating, having no babe to nurse. But the supply had slowly diminished. Doctor Phillips said it would take around a week to ten days after the birth for her milk to dry up. Well, it was day nine, so thankfully it wouldn't be much longer.

Her heart squeezed as grief overwhelmed her once again. The breastmilk was the last physical connection she had with her pregnancy. Soon her body would bear no trace that she'd carried a baby in her belly. Not even a single stretch mark.

CHAPTER ELEVEN

TYLER OPENED his eyes and stared at the ceiling for a while before slowly rolling over to gaze at Hope, still asleep. She'd tossed and turned for a while last night. Finally she'd gone to the bathroom and not long after, had become restful. She must've taken a sleeping tablet. She did that most nights. Tyler worried that she'd form an addiction, but for now they gave her some respite. Sleep would help her heal, find rest for her soul—at least for a few hours.

Five and a half weeks had passed since they'd buried their son. Hope had spent that time so deep in mourning, he wondered if he'd ever be able to reach her again. Would he see her smile again?

Tyler had feared leaving her when the time came to return to work. Perhaps it was a godsend that she was always still asleep when he left. He used the time in the car on the way to the office, to pray for Hope, asking God to let her morning be spent in slumber. He'd catch up with his team at the office for a few hours—making sure to call Hope a few times once he was certain she would be awake.

Not that long ago, she would have laughed at the phone calls and said something like, "Checking up on me, eh?" Now all he got was an unenthusiastic "I'm fine", when he knew she was anything but.

Around two-thirty, he'd return home and work from there for the rest of the day. He always found Hope in the same place—slumped in the armchair in the nursery, staring at the empty crib. Perhaps they should redecorate the room, turn it into another guest room. But he was too uncertain whether it would be the right thing to do. What if the nursery was her place of healing? What if all she needed was time, and he was too impatient with the process?

Besides, any spare time he found, he'd used to strip the bathroom of its wallpaper. After Hope's episode, he'd had no choice but to clean up the walls and paint them.

Glancing over his shoulder toward the bedside pedestal, Tyler checked the time on the digital clock. Almost eight a.m. They'd missed the Easter sunrise service, but there was still the normal Sunday service they could attend starting at nine. Would Hope go? He'd asked her last night. The only response he'd received to his question was a non-committal shrug.

They needed to get back to church, their support structure. Those people were praying for them and could help them heal. And he was also in desperate need of healing. He hurt just as much. He'd suffered a great loss too. It had been hell these past few weeks trying to keep everything together because his wife had fallen apart.

Tyler shook Hope's shoulder gently.

She stirred and slowly opened her eyes. Frowning, she mumbled, "What?"

"Hope, honey, it's Easter Sunday. I thought perhaps we could go to church today. It's been a while."

Her eyes clamped shut, and she shook her head. "I don't want to go."

"Hope, we can't stop living just because—"

He paused. Probably wise not to speak the words.

Hope shot up in bed. "Because what, Tyler? Because our son died?" She'd raised her voice. "What's 'just' about that?"

Tyler eased up in the bed too. Taking her hand in his, he gave it a light squeeze. "Look I'm hurting too, but life goes on. If we let Him, God will give us the strength to endure this pain. He also lost a son—He knows what we're going through."

Hope flung her pillow across the room. It collided with the dresser, knocking some perfume bottles over. One rolled off the edge and fell onto the carpet.

"I. Don't. Care." Anger fouled her tone. "He's God. He could handle it. *And* His son was raised from the dead!"

Drawing a deep breath, she buried her head in her hands. "I... I'm just a woman who had hopes and dreams for a happy family. Now—" She sucked back a sob, swiping away her tears with the back of her hand. "God and I are done with. Finished. He took my son from me. I can't forgive Him for that."

She stared at Tyler, her eyes devoid of emotion. "It wasn't only my baby who died that day. My soul died too."

Hope could hear herself saying the words, but it was as if someone else was speaking them, and she merely looked on from a distance. Had she really said that? Worse, did she mean it?

Turning her back on Tyler, she shrank back under the sheet. "I'd like to be alone."

The covers landed on Hope as Tyler threw them back and surged out of bed. Sucking his breath in and out, he stomped across the bedroom. "One day you'll have to snap out of this, Hope, and face the world again. I only pray that by then it's not too late for us." He slammed the bedroom door shut behind him.

Her eyes stung and her throat tightened. How had things gone so terribly wrong for them? How could Tyler love her anymore? She was repulsive. She'd been the one responsible for their baby's death, and although he didn't say it, she knew that's what Tyler was thinking. And she'd just had the gall to blame God for Matty's death.

But He could have prevented it.

Yes, God could have. So why hadn't He? He was all-powerful. All-knowing. Present everywhere. He could've done something to prevent her from going to work that day.

But she'd known there were risks. And still, she'd chosen to get into the tank with a distressed dolphin. Had she really thought the dolphin birth could go off without a single problem?

Stupid.

Guilty.

Woman.

The bedroom door opened. Any minute now, Tyler would wrap his arms around her and say he was sorry for what he'd said. Would she have it within her to say she was sorry too?

His closet door opened, shutting with a dull thud moments later.

She peered over the covers. He was getting dressed? In his Sunday best?

Oh, let him go. Let him be with God, and leave her alone in her misery. Clearly she wasn't a priority. He didn't love her anymore. He didn't want to be with her. And who could blame him? She had killed his son.

Inside Clearwater Chapel, Tyler reached for the seat beside him, ominously empty. Until a few weeks ago, his beautiful wife had occupied it every Sunday without fail, except, of course, when there was a storm of epic proportions. And one of a different kind had unleashed itself in their home. The place where they were supposed to live happily ever after, raise a family, grow old together, had become a house destined for destruction.

It had been hard to leave Hope as he had this morning, but he was desperate to be in the Lord's house today. If only she'd joined him, reconnected with God as he was doing.

During the praise and worship time, heartache hemmed Tyler in on all sides. He couldn't shake the thought of how abandoned Hope must be feeling right now. Why couldn't he have just kept it together earlier?

Contending not only with his anguish, doubt gnawed at the peace he sought. He should've stayed at home with her. Already she believed that God had forsaken her—did she need to think that he had too? He had to admit that there were times when he felt the same way as Hope. That was why it had been so important for him to come to the morning service. If he was to remain strong for Hope, he needed God's strength to empower him daily and give him wisdom. He couldn't do this grieving thing, and this supporting-your-spouse-through-the-worst-time-of your-lives thing, on his own.

Back in church where he could release every pent up emotion of the past six weeks, every pretense of coping to his Maker, Tyler wept.

For his son.

For his marriage.

For being disconnected from God since Hope lost the baby. Instead of running to Him for comfort, Tyler had somberly remained in limbo in the shadow of the valley of death.

Today, that would all change. He would cling to God with all his might. If he led the way forward by example, perhaps Hope would follow and find her way back to her Savior...back to her first love for Jesus.

And him.

Tyler sobbed uncontrollably as communion was served, the enormity of God's sacrifice of His only son suddenly too real. He had only held his lifeless son for a few minutes after he was born, yet he knew the loss of little Matty would forever be raw. But God the Father had walked and talked and communed with his Son since long before the beginning of time. Still, He gave Him up freely. All to save a wretched people.

Like him.

Like Hope.

Yes, even an innocent babe like Matty.

All are born into sin. No one is righteous.

Eyes tightly shut, Tyler slipped the small piece of bread he'd squashed between his fingers past his lips.

Thank You, Father, for sending Your son. Thank you, Jesus, for being willing to die.

Suffer the little children to come unto me.

Oh, Lord, I know how much you love children, please take little Matty into Your arms and give him a great big hug and a kiss from his daddy. Tell him I love and miss him so much. As does his mommy...she's just too broken at the moment to ask You herself.

A shoulder pressed against his.

Tyler groaned inwardly, not ready to give up the privacy an empty row had afforded him. He cracked one eye open to see who had claimed the seat beside him...this late in the service.

Will Martin.

"Hey, buddy," Will whispered as he slid an arm around Tyler's shoulder and pulled him into a side hug. "It's good to see you at church today."

"You too."

Will had been a pillar of strength at Matty's funeral. And just before Tyler carried the tiny coffin out of the church, Diana, Will's wife, had sung such a beautiful song. Her words, *I'll hold you forever in heaven*, had flooded him with the knowledge and hope that laying Matty's fragile body in the ground wasn't the end of his son's life.

It was only the beginning!

After the cup had been served, Pastor Reynolds, a visiting preacher, brought a powerful message from the book of Job. Tyler soaked up every single word. If only Hope had been there to listen—it wouldn't sound nearly as mind-blowing told to her secondhand when he got home. That's if she would even hear him out.

The preacher spoke of being thankful for our pain because it's in times of suffering that we can experience God's strength and grace in ways we never could have before.

Coming to a close, the seasoned pastor leaned on the pulpit and stared down at the congregation before his face brightened into a smile so wide one could be forgiven for thinking heaven itself had painted it there.

"My grace is sufficient for you, for my power is made perfect in weakness. Therefore I will boast all the more gladly about my weaknesses, so that Christ's power may rest on me," he said. "Pain, my friends, awakens the believer to God."

He reached for the glass of water on the pulpit and took a long drink.

Tyler was certain the preacher's pause was deliberate, allowing the congregation to dwell on his words.

Setting the glass back down, Pastor Reynolds continued. "What is your weakness today? A long, drawn-out illness? A sudden one? The loss of a family member—a parent, a sibling, a child? A barren womb and an empty crib? Financial difficulties? Employment problems? Homelessness? Loneliness? Can you trust God with your pain? Can you say, like Job, 'though he slay me, yet will I hope in him'?"

The words instantly reminded Tyler of a thought he'd had one night in the shower just a few months ago.

Would you still praise Me if any of that was taken from you?

Had God been preparing him for what was to come?

"In closing," the preacher said as he shut his Bible, "pain without a purpose, is just unadulterated suffering. Eternity is what makes the difference for the Christian. You see, our years on earth are merely a preparation for the life that is to come. And sometimes, as C. S. Lewis puts it, God has to shout to us in our pain to get our attention to return to Him, to get us to allow Him to shape us into His image."

He paused and smiled again. "My brothers and sisters, it isn't difficult to find God—all you have to do is follow the cross. And remember that in all things, God works for the good of those who love him, who have been called according to his purpose."

Yes, Lord, yes. I will follow you. I will trust You. I will praise You…in the good times and in the bad.

Tyler's spirits had lifted. Truly he'd met with God today. He couldn't wait to share with Hope what had happened, and what the pastor's sermon was all about.

Back home, he tiptoed upstairs, unsure if he'd find Hope still asleep in bed, or where he usually found her—in the nursery.

He popped his head around the door to Matty's room first. As expected, Hope sat in the armchair, gaze fixed on the crib. She clutched a baby blanket to her chest, something she hadn't done before. Was this progression? Or regression? He had no idea, but feared the latter.

When would the medication she'd been prescribed for her post-partum depression start helping her? The psychiatrist had said it would take six weeks to steady the serotonin levels in her brain, and that she would need to be on the meds for at least a year to stabilize before she could be weaned off the treatment.

Any day now he should see signs of the girl he married emerging from the dark places she seemed to go to.

He neared. Dropping to his knees in front of Hope, he took her hands in his. "Hi, honey."

She turned to look at him through red-rimmed eyes.

Tyler pressed his lips to the back of her hand. "I'm so sorry for the way I treated you this morning. I should never have gotten upset with you."

Her face remained emotionless. She blinked, slowly, lethargically.

"But although I'm sorry I left you alone, I'm not sorry I went to church." His mouth curved in a smile. "Oh Hope, I met with God in such an amazing way. There was a visiting speaker, and it was as if that sermon was for me alone. I wish you could have been th—"

"I'm sorry, too, *ku'uipo*," Hope said, almost mechanically.

Tyler's heart soared. She hadn't called him sweetheart since that fateful Valentine's Day.

"I'm going to be a better wife to you."

He waited for a smile from her. He missed the way her grin used to spread from one side of her face to the other.

It never came.

Patience. He had to exercise it. One day she *would* smile and laugh again.

"Would you like to visit Matty's grave this afternoon, place some flowers there? You haven't been out of the house since our very first visit."

She offered him an uncertain nod.

Tyler tried not to get too excited. There was a big chance she'd no longer be willing to go by the time they were ready to leave. It had happened before.

"Why don't I make us some tea and a bite to eat? Then I'll help you to get dressed, and we can leave."

CHAPTER TWELVE

WHILE HE waited for the eggs to cook on the stove behind him, Tyler stared out of the kitchen window across the sparkling blue pool, lost in thought.

Over the past five weeks, Hope had tried hard to return to normality. She'd actually had a few good days. It was during those times that he thought her medication might finally be starting to take effect. Or his prayers were reaching heaven. Unfortunately, the difficult days far outweighed the good ones. Still, he was grateful for the periods that did offer them both a respite.

His chest tightened. Would his wife ever be the same again?

Would he?

He still loved Hope so much, and he wanted to see her well again, but Satan kept hounding him with the lie that their marriage wouldn't last...that Tyler couldn't last. *Sooner or later you will snap and leave*, the evil one taunted.

There was no ignoring the fact that the illness in Hope's mind had dug its vile claws so deep inside of her these past three months, making the escape she desperately sought almost impossible. Some days, he could literally see the darkness overtaking her, and any efforts to live normally, be normal, quickly vanished as she disappeared into the downward spiraling black hole.

Shaking his head, he blew out a defeated breath as he turned back to the stove. Tyler Peterson, marine engineer extraordinaire. He could build robots—large and small—that could probe the depths of the ocean. If only he could create a device that could analyze the abyss that had claimed Hope, then spit out the information he needed to make her better.

A few days before, Hope had opened up to him for the very first time, describing the black hole feeling as well as everything else she'd been struggling with since Matty died. Sadness, hopelessness, helplessness, worthlessness, guilt were all part of her waking hours. She had zero energy, was constantly fatigued, and had lost so much weight that her clothes hung on her like sacks. Tyler constantly struggled to get her to eat something. She didn't want to see anyone, didn't want to talk to anyone. All she wanted most days, she admitted, was to be left alone in her dark place.

Tyler had tried to get her to go back to church—if she could just commune with God again, confide in a friend—Diana perhaps—it would help her so much to heal. But Hope had refused, although she didn't begrudge him going to church. In fact, she'd encouraged it. Probably so she could be in her alone space.

Since the miscarriage, people had called—in person and telephonically. He'd never realized there were so many people who cared about them. But Tyler always had to make an apology on Hope's behalf. Even the cards and notes they sent or left, she showed no interest in reading.

Since that Easter Sunday when he'd had an encounter with God, he'd spent hours reading up on Hope's disorder so that he could understand everything his wife was going through. He felt God was leading him to do all he could to understand her illness. That way he'd be better equipped to help her. Tyler didn't like what he read, and he feared for Hope. The more he read, the more he wondered whether there *was* anything he could do. On top of the feelings of helplessness, his research had opened him up to horrible questions, and he found himself asking questions too—had she been plagued with thoughts of death or suicide as so many suffering from depression do? Hope never said, and he was too scared to ask for fear of putting the idea into her head if she hadn't.

The eggs and bacon cooked, Tyler dished up two plates and set them down on a tray. He filled two glasses with orange juice before dashing into the dining room to pinch a red rose from the bouquet adorning the table. Every weekend, he'd place a fresh bunch of flowers in the house, hoping they would lift Hope's spirits.

He returned to the kitchen and placed the rose in a slender vase which he had filled with water.

The tray now adorned with the bloom, an expression of his love, Tyler was ready to take the food upstairs. But before he could, Hope dragged herself into the kitchen.

"Morning," she mumbled. "What are you doing at home? It *is* Monday, isn't it?"

"I took the day off because…" Stupid. Shut up. Don't remind her what day it is.

Hope slid onto a stool on the other side of the island. She leaned her head to the side, resting her cheek on her hand, and eyed him. "Because this is the day Matty should have been born?"

Confound it, too late.

He swallowed hard and offered a slight nod.

He should change the subject.

"Coffee?" Without waiting for her to say yes or no, Tyler swung around and poured a cup of fresh brew. He added milk then set the hot drink down on the counter in front of Hope.

"Thank you." She flicked a glance his way before focusing on her cup. Lifting it to her mouth, Hope took a swig. She jerked the cup away, spilling dark liquid down her pajama top.

Narrowed eyes flashed an annoyed look. "What the—? Did the devil pitchfork this coffee?" she snapped.

"I'm sorry, honey. I don't understand, the coffee didn't feel that hot." He'd certainly made it the same way he had a thousand times before. He rushed to the sink and grabbed a damp cloth. He tried to clean the spill from the flowery blue fabric, but Hope shoved his hand away.

"Just leave it," she said, her words clipped.

Tyler held out a palm to her. "Stay right there, honey. I'll get you a clean top."

Leaving her in the kitchen, Tyler raced upstairs.

He opened the first drawer in the highboy. Seeing Hope's make-up and jewelry, he shut the drawer and opened the second one. Bras and panties waved back at him. He tried the third one.

Her T-shirts.

Yes, jackpot.

Now, which one would she like to wear? The slightest thing often triggered Hope, sending her into a downward spiral. So he wanted to be careful not to make the wrong choice.

Tyler flipped through the neatly stacked shirts that hadn't been worn since before that fateful day. Some days, Hope either didn't get out of her pajamas—skipping the daily shower she used to love so much—or she'd slop around in the one or two jeans and T-shirts she seemed to favor.

Her work shirts were all stacked on the far right-hand side of the drawer he rummaged through.

As he got to the bottom of the pile on the left, his fingers brushed up against something cardboardy. He pulled out a box, about the size of his palm, and examined it. Hope's monthly supply of sertraline, the SSRI medication for her depression. For April. It was now May. Why had Hope buried this beneath her clothes? Unless she was trying to hide it.

He opened the box to a full month's supply of medicine. Fingers trembling, Tyler dropped it on the shirts then shoved his hand beneath the stack of folded fabric again. He pulled out two more boxes.

March and May's supplies.

Clutching the three boxes between his fingers, he rushed to the bathroom. The same packaging perched on the shelf above Hope's basin. He set the medicine down on the granite countertop, then reached for the one on display and flipped the box around to check the label. His pulse accelerated. The label was dated February 15th—the day after Matty's stillbirth...the day she first met with her psychiatrist.

Opening the box, he counted the remaining pills in their blister packaging. Five. With three untouched filled prescriptions, and one not quite finished yet, Tyler quickly put two and two together. Hope hadn't even taken the medication for a month. No wonder she was struggling to get well again.

Failing to contain his outrage, Tyler scooped up all four boxes and headed back downstairs. His heart pounded harder and harder against his ribs the closer he got to the kitchen.

As he entered, Hope slowly raised her head. Red-rimmed eyes stared blankly at him.

Inhaling and exhaling far too rapidly, Tyler came to a dead stop beside Hope, nostrils flaring. He let the boxes fall onto the counter in front of Hope then pointed at them. "Care to explain?" A tremor warbled his voice.

Hope shifted her gaze to the identical packs, then back to Tyler again. She blinked, her lashes meeting at a funereal pace. She looked so terribly tired and weary.

Instinctively he wanted to apologize. Perhaps he'd come across too harsh, practically dropping his findings into her lap. Especially on a day like today.

Then again, maybe he'd been too soft and accommodating all these months, trying so hard to tiptoe around her. What if a little tough love was exactly what was needed in this situation?

He blew out a heavy sigh. Who knew? He could only try, because what he'd been doing up until now, had proved ineffective.

Why, oh why hadn't she just flushed those pills away and disposed of the empty boxes? What had possessed her to keep them all?

"I…" Hope cast her gaze to the floor, her brain too tired, too foggy to think of an excuse. Besides, what explanation could she possibly give? The facts stared her, and Tyler, in the face. He knew she'd stopped taking her sertraline meds. And unless the next words that came out of her mouth were the hard, cold truth, he'd know she was lying.

She raised her gaze and their eyes locked. "I–I haven't been taking the medication. I–I took it for the first three weeks, but it made me feel ill. I'm sorry, but I couldn't continue with it any longer."

"Hope…" Tyler's voice softened. He wrapped his arms around her, and she buried her head against his chest. "Honey, your doctor said it would take at least six weeks for everything to equalize. You were halfway there. Maybe the side effects would've disappeared once your serotonin levels were rectified. Did you speak with your psychiatrist about the side effects? And more importantly, did you tell her you were stopping?"

She shook her head. "I just wanted the tremors, and the sleeplessness, and the nausea to go away. I thought, with time, I could get better on my own. Once I'd grieved enough."

Tyler's hand brushed up and down her back. "Honey, we will always grieve. We lost a child, it's inevitable. There won't come a day when we'll suddenly say 'Now we've cried for long enough. We're done.' But in time, I guarantee it won't hurt nearly as much as it does right now. Together, we can learn to live in this new normal without our little boy. Let's not drift apart, Hope, because I couldn't bear to lose you too."

"I–I don't w–want to be l–lost…" But she had no control over the darkness that had far too often beckoned her into its kingdom.

Placing a hand gently beneath her chin, Tyler tipped her head. "I've been thinking that maybe it would be a good idea for you to return to work next month. You could start with just a few hours a day, until you feel you're able to manage a full day. This sitting around, doing uh…little…when you've always been an active person—physically, mentally, and spiritually—isn't good for you. It's feeding your depression."

Work? Seriously? Was she ready? Could she face being back where her nightmare began?

"I–I don't know. I'll have to think about it."

"All right, honey, that's a start." Tyler's gaze perused the cold food. "Well, that meal's spoiled. Those eggs will be rubbery now and the bacon tough and chewy."

His breath hitched. "I have an idea. Why don't you get dressed, and I'll take you down to Pier 60? We can have a late breakfast. Afterwards, we can take a long walk on the beach. It'll be good for your soul, I promise. Just trust me."

Fearing to venture outside amongst strangers, everything inside of Hope started to tremble. But she had to try even harder to integrate with society once more. Somewhere, sometime, she had to start living again. If not for her sake, then for her husband's. She might not deserve better than this, but he certainly did.

CHAPTER THIRTEEN

HOPE SAT inside her Jeep, clutching the steering wheel as she stared at the entrance of the rescue center. How many times had she run through those glass doors, eager to do a day's work, unable to wait to be with her sea babies?

Now she needed wild horses to drag her inside.

Tyler had wanted to take another day off work to be here with her. She had insisted that it wasn't necessary—this wasn't the first day of school, and she wasn't five. But as her heart pounded, blood throbbing in her ears as it pulsed through her veins, she wished she did have Tyler's hand to hold.

It had taken her nearly a week after Tyler suggested she returned to work to make the decision to go back. And another three weeks psyching herself up for this day. Thankfully the pleasant memory of that long walk on the beach she and Tyler had taken kept returning, giving her the strength to do this.

She missed the ocean.

She missed the aquarium.

She missed just being normal.

Perhaps the catalyst to her healing would be working with her beloved sea creatures again, being out on the sea.

Face your demons people often said, without a clue how difficult that was for the one navigating the dark. Being back at the rescue center, there'd certainly be no avoiding the devils she'd been hiding from these past few months.

At least, not for long.

The aquarium doors opened and Ethan raced down the stairs toward her Jeep.

Hope wanted to start the vehicle and slam it into reverse. She wasn't ready for this.

Instead, she tightened her grip on the wheel, remaining motionless like one of those crash test dummies.

Ethan flung her door open and bent his tall frame halfway inside the cabin to give her a hug. His face beamed. "Hope! I'm so happy to see you again."

Hope froze and Ethan quickly released her. He straightened then draped his arm casually over the top of the open door. "Gosh, I have missed you, although I had to learn really fast in your absence, what with no replacement vet available. It was good practice for my final exams though, which, by the way, I finished writing last week. And aced." He held out a palm to high-five her.

She pried the fingers of one hand from the wheel and pressed her palm lightly against his.

"Hey, I came around to your house a few times during my lunch times to see how you were doing," he continued. "Never did find you at home. Maybe you were out shopping or at a doctor's appointment. Gosh, I hope you weren't sleeping. Sorry if you were and I woke you."

Nope, she was there. And she wasn't asleep. She'd seen him from her bedroom window, just as she'd seen Diana, and Sandy, and the many other friends and church people who had come around to visit her. Sometimes Tyler had handled their intrusions.

Eventually they'd all grown weary of trying to see her and had stopped coming to her door. Maybe her husband had asked them to stay away for a time.

"I'm so sorry about what happened to you and Tyler and the baby. I should have told you not to get inside the tank that day. Insisted. I feel responsible."

Tears stung, and Hope blinked them away as she looked up at her colleague. "Don't. It's not your fault, Ethan. Not in the slightest. You know how stubborn I can be—there's no way I would've listened to anything you might've said."

He pursed his lips and nodded. "I came to the funeral. It was a beautiful service."

"Thank you." The cabin suddenly closed in on her. She had to get out of there.

Hope swung her legs out of the Jeep, and Ethan took two steps back. She forced a frozen smile to her lips as she pushed to her feet. "Shall we get to work?"

Ethan grinned and shut the door behind her. "Ab-so-lu-te-ly."

The closer they got to the doors, the faster her pulse beat, like the pounding of *pahu* drums. She forced one foot in front of the other. "So, aced the exams? I'm proud of you."

"It's thanks to you, Hope. You've been a great mentor." Ethan pressed his palm against the glass door to open it. He allowed Hope to pass through before following her inside.

It felt surreal to be back and she pinched her arm just to make sure she wasn't dreaming.

"Joon will be glad to see you. She's almost due." Ethan rolled his eyes. His head flopped backward and he released a groan to the rafters. "I'm so sorry. I shouldn't have—"

Hope reached out and wrapped her fingers around his arm. "Don't. It's okay. Y–you can't tiptoe around me. I'm here to work and pregnant dolphins are a part of what we do here." Although not that frequently.

She sucked in a deep breath then exhaled slowly. "Let's try to get through each day as normally as we can. All right? What I'm trying to say is, don't treat me differently."

Ethan nodded. "Okay. In that case, do you want to see Val?"

"Val?" Who on earth was that? A new employee? A turtle? A seal?

"The dolphin. We named her Val on account of the fact that we rescued her on Valentine's Day."

The dolphin? The one responsible for her child's death. No way was she ready to face that demon yet.

Hope paused. More like her feet didn't want to move. "S–she's still here?"

"Yes. We feared for her in the beginning. She was really depressed during those first few weeks. But she's a lot better now. Time has helped her to heal. She's such a survivor." Ethan chuckled as he took a step forward, then paused because Hope still stood rooted to the spot. "Valentine's Day aside, we definitely gave her the right name because Val means strong, valiant, or the fierce one."

Fierce one was the right description. Hope and her baby had felt the backlash of that tail as she'd thrashed in the water.

Then again, Hope herself had groaned at the pain of childbirth, although her agony was more emotional than physical. The baby she'd had to birth was so small, weighing a mere two pounds. Not like giving birth to a full-term babe, or calf as Val had, who wasn't alive to do their part in the birthing process. Could she blame the dolphin then for having flailed her body in those last moments before the dead pup was yanked from her body? Hope had merely been in the wrong place at the wrong time…a place she'd willingly placed herself.

Ethan's voice drew her back to the present, away from that

fateful moment. And from responding to the siren's call that beckoned her back into the darkness.

"…so we do plan to release her back into the wild fairly soon. Do you want to see how she's doing?"

"Um, maybe another day, okay?" She pasted on a smile. "Take me to see Benny and Joon. And Sandy."

CHAPTER FOURTEEN

DURING HER first month back at work, Hope had only spent a few hours each day at the aquarium, returning home most days before two. From the beginning of June, however, she'd decided to try and stay for the entire day. Almost three weeks now and she was coping. For the most part. At least, that's what everyone believed.

Work had been healing, though not to the degree or as fast as Hope would've liked. Sometimes she had to force herself to go in, and other days she couldn't wait to get there. Every day, whether good or bad, she still battled her rollercoaster emotions, and she still fought against the constant fatigue—though no one would've guessed. Not her colleagues, nor the wonderful husband whom she didn't deserve. And she planned to keep it that way. If everyone thought she was doing well, nobody would expend their energy trying to fix her. If *she* couldn't pull herself out of the mire of depression, what chance did they stand?

She still hadn't attended a church service. Most Sundays, Tyler attended. Alone. He didn't push her though. He got it that she was angry with God and working that anger out was between her and

God. He'd stopped trying to be the mediator—that was Jesus' position, and His Spirit would draw her back to the Father, he'd said the last time he asked Hope to go to church with him.

The bedroom was the most difficult place to keep up a pretense. Hope's mental state had eroded any desire for intimacy. But Tyler had needs, and she was his wife, though she had to fight hard not to allow resentment to destroy her. Did she fool Tyler the infrequent times they made love? Or did her performance in the bedroom tip him off that all was still not well with his wife? Perhaps she managed to deceive him, and perhaps he merely chose not to make a big deal out of it for fear of opening a can of worms that neither of them would be able to close.

Her phone rang as she grabbed her rescue center T-shirt from the drawer. She pulled the shirt over her head and made a dive for the phone where it lay on the bed. She snatched it up and checked the screen.

Ethan.

Hope held the device to her ear. "You're calling rather early, aren't you? What's up, besides you?"

Ethan whooped with excitement. "Joon is in labor! Her breathing is irregular, she's arching and flexing and swimming upside down. You know these things can go as speedily as half an hour, so get your butt down here now."

"Or as long as six hours, Ethan." She'd wondered yesterday when Joon's appetite had decreased, whether it was time.

"Yes, Hope, or as long. But would you want to risk missing this event?"

Did she? Truthfully, she had no idea. On the one hand she wanted to be there when Joon gave birth. The dolphin had been a part of her life for nearly two years. And as she'd diagnosed the pregnancy, she kind of felt like the cow's obstetrician. But on the other hand...if anything went wrong during the birth, she'd probably fall apart. Then everyone would know the horrible truth—Hope Peterson wasn't even close to being whole again.

She huffed out a sigh. "All right. I'll be there in fifteen minutes. Keep a close eye on her."

"Yes, ma'am."

She was about to cut the call when she paused. "Butt? Getting rather cocky now that you've qualified, aren't you?"

A low laugh rumbled through the phone. "See you soon."

Hope hung up and grabbed her backpack from where she'd set it down on the floor against the wall next to her bed, then headed downstairs to the kitchen where Tyler had made coffee and toast.

Seeing her enter, he smiled. "Honey, you're just in time. Sit."

"Can't. Joon's in labor. I need to get to the center."

Tiny wrinkles formed on Tyler's brow. "Are you up to handling a dolphin birth?"

She had no idea, but she was about to find out.

With a nod, Hope pecked Tyler on the cheek before grabbing a slice of toast from one of the plates and giving it a light spread of butter. "I'll take this to go. See you later, *ku'uipo*. Don't forget to lock up when you leave." Usually, Tyler was the first one out of the house in the morning and she'd do the locking up. Not today.

She rushed outside through the back door and hopped into her Jeep.

At the rescue center, Hope found Sandy and Ethan pacing the pavement beside the pool like expectant parents. Joon swam through the water rapidly, flexing her body upward then crunching it as the contractions forced the calf through the birth canal. Already the flukes and half the tail were visible. Any moment now, that calf would plop out into the water and start swimming next to its mother.

Benny glided along near Joon, watching and waiting for his offspring to be born.

It was a beautiful sight.

No. It was an agonizing sight. Tyler had never had his chance to pace beside her hospital bed, anxious for the moment she'd be wheeled into the delivery room, listening for their baby's cry. Instead, still reeling from the traumatic news they'd just received, they'd been rushed to the delivery room where Hope's body had to expel her stillborn baby.

She closed her eyes, willing herself not to fall apart, not to remember, not to go back to the darkness.

Not today.

Not now.

But it was hard to stay strong.

A cheer sounded close by, and Hope opened her eyes just in time to see the pink cloud in the water before it dissipated. Joon swam away from the blood, her calf slipstreaming beside her as they rose to the surface for the young dolphin to get its first breath of fresh air. What an incredible bond they already shared.

The calf chin-slapped the water, facilitating the breathing process, before following its mother for another swimming lesson.

Close by, Benny swished through water.

Out on the pavement, Ethan and Sandy had wrapped their arms around each other, whooping and cheering as they danced in a circle. Only for a brief moment. Realizing what they were doing, the closeness of the moment, they quickly moved away from each other.

Sandy leaned forward to gaze into the water as she rubbed her hands together. "Isn't that just the most glorious thing you've ever seen?"

Despite Hope's personal sadness, it was a beautiful sight, and she gazed upon the new family with wonder for quite some time, her racing heart finally slowing to normal.

All day long as they monitored Joon and her calf, Hope's gaze drifted toward the far tank she'd painstakingly avoided since returning to work. For seven weeks she'd refused to go near Val's tank, wouldn't even glance in that direction. Today, she was intrigued. That dolphin had gone through what Hope had—worse, as her baby was full term—and had survived.

How had Val managed to do that? How had she found the will to continue living?

During her studies and years as a vet, Hope had read various reports about dolphins committing suicide. Of course, there were people who believed that cetaceans didn't have the brainpower to commit suicide, but stories, and science, suggested that dolphin suicide was real. Even Pliny the Elder—Roman author, naturalist, and natural philosopher—wrote about such an account in the 1st century AD in his book *Naturalis Historiae*. She'd found that fascinating. Far more recently—if one could call thirty-four years ago recent—Kathy, one of the bottlenose dolphins trained for the '60s television show *Flipper*, swam into her trainer's arms, held her breath, and ended her life.

There were so many days when Hope had wanted to end it all herself. But how could she do that to Tyler? So she held on, sometimes by the thinnest of threads, teetering at the edge of this life and the next.

And somehow, always managing to hide her precipice from those around her.

Taking a last glance at the new dolphin family, Hope turned away and ambled across to the next pool where four seals played. She continued on past, coming to a stop at the platform overhanging Val's pool. Her heart pounded. The last time Hope had seen this dolphin was shortly after she'd been thwacked in the stomach by its powerful tail.

She went down on her knees and swirled her fingers through the water.

The dolphin swam toward Hope, then veered away, heading back the way she'd come. Did she sense who Hope was? Did she blame her for the death of her calf, as Hope blamed her for the death of her baby? Hope had been there to help the dolphin give birth, but there was nothing she could do except assist in removing the dead pup from her belly. If the mother had been found earlier, maybe there might've been a chance of helping her to birth a live calf.

The similarities between Hope and Val were staggering. But if she didn't feel she was to blame for the death of Val's calf, was it really fair for her to accuse God and place the responsibility of Matty's death on His shoulders? If she hadn't been so stubborn after the accident, insisting that she was okay... If she'd gone to the hospital, or Doctor Phillips, instead of heading home and sleeping...perhaps then they could've saved her baby.

Once again, tears came uninvited. They dripped down Hope's cheeks, falling into the water below as she curled forward into a fetal position.

Suddenly, Val broke through the surface in front of Hope. Paddling her fluke, the dolphin pushed herself out of the water, standing upright like a performer in a dolphin show. Her head bounced up and down, and she emitted clicking sounds and whistles from her toothed beak, although they sounded more like squeaks and squawks.

The dolphin fell back into the water, swimming away once again before returning. Head sticking out of the water, she stared at Hope through pitchy eyes, her mouth open as she tried to communicate. Was the dolphin apologizing to her for what had happened? It certainly seemed so.

Hope stretched her hand forward, and Val nudged her nose into Hope's palm. And in that single touch, something extraordinary happened. The resentment toward the dolphin that Hope had grappled with melted away.

Hope's loud sob broke the silence.

And then a hand squeezed her shoulder.

"Hope? Are you all right?"

Ethan.

She swiped the moisture away from her cheeks and eyes with the back of her hand. "I... For so long, I've hated her. But t–today I realized that she's been through the same hurt, the same pain, the same loss, as I have."

"And just look at her now." Ethan beamed. "She's a fighter. And so are you."

Hope didn't feel like a fighter. Not one bit.

The dolphin swam away. It was only then that Hope noticed the row of pink star-shaped scars on her side, just in front of her left pectoral fin. An old wound that had healed, a shark bite perhaps. Maybe even an aggressive male whose advances she hadn't been receptive to.

"Hope, we have plans in place to return Val to her natural habitat tomorrow—in the vicinity where we found her. I haven't told you because you never seemed to want to speak about her. But it seems as if your feelings might've changed today. So, would you like to come and help with Val's release?"

Would it help to free her as well?

"I–I think I'd like that." Tagging along the following day seemed like a good idea.

CHAPTER FIFTEEN

ALMOST TWO months had passed since the rescue team had released Val back into the sea at Pass-A-Grille beach, right beside the southwest jetty. Several curious holiday-makers had wandered down from the main beach to see what was going on.

Standing in the surf on that hot summer's day, a strange sadness had overwhelmed Hope as she watched the dolphin's gray body wiggle through the waves and disappear into the clear, blue ocean. Although Hope was always despondent—had been that way for seven months now—it was a different kind of sadness on that particular day.

Just as today brought its own unique reason for her sorrow.

Leaving Tyler to sleep in a little longer—after all, wasn't that what Saturdays were for?—she forced herself to quietly slip out from between the sheets and tiptoed down the passage to the bathroom. Perhaps if she could deal in secret with the thoughts that had ravaged her mind all night, she could turn the skies from black to blue today. Not outside, but deep in her mind.

Hope stared at herself in the mirror. How she had aged in just a few months. Tyler constantly reminded her that she was still as beautiful as the day he'd fallen in love with her. But he was just saying that so she wouldn't feel so bad about herself. He couldn't possibly mean it.

She rubbed her hands over her drawn cheeks, then stared at her thin fingers and arms. Who could love a skeleton like her? A corpse… No, a zombie, for most days she was no better than the walking dead.

On the really bad weeks, Tyler would try to convince her to see Doctor Montrose again. And to go back on the medication and stick to it this time.

But she just couldn't.

Would it take hitting rock bottom for her to follow Tyler's advice? Or had she already been to the deepest depths, and was ever so slowly making her way back to the surface of sanity?

Squatting down on her haunches, Hope rummaged in the cabinet beneath the basin. Hard to believe that exactly a year ago, she and Tyler had stood in a different, smaller bathroom, eagerly awaiting the best news they'd ever received. If she were ever to hear that news again, she'd spend the eight months that followed in a perpetual state of worry, too afraid to do a thing.

Her fingers wrapped around the slender shape she sought. Thankful that she'd kept the used test as a memento, Hope clutched it tightly. She retreated and sank to the floor.

As she stared at the two blue lines, still visible after a year, her world shattered all over again, and she wept. Some days she wished they had bought a house with an en suite bathroom.

Today was not one of those days.

Here, away from her bedroom, she could weep freely.

Raising her face toward the ceiling, Hope closed her eyes and watched as the dark clouds rolled in.

Were those muffled sobs he heard?

Tyler rolled over to an empty bed. Certainly not the first time, and it would unfortunately not be the last. He and Hope had gotten through several firsts, with more to come. They'd survived coming home from the hospital with empty arms, the due date, the first visit to the grave, and Hope returning to work. They would survive today's first as well, although he could already tell it wouldn't be pleasant.

This time a year ago, they'd been so excited, oblivious that a storm worse than the one lashing their apartment windows, would turn their world upside down only a few short months later.

He rose and hurried to the bathroom. The door was shut, and Tyler prayed it wasn't locked this time. Despite reassuring himself that they would get through all the difficult days and would eventually experience the healing God would bring, his heart still beat wildly every time he stood in front of a closed door with Hope sobbing on the other side. What if she had a day where she could simply no longer cope? What if one day she just decided to give up? What if the day came when he would find her limp, lifeless body on the other side of that wooden divide?

He has sent me to bring beauty instead of ashes, the oil of joy instead of mourning, a garment of praise instead of a spirit of despair.

No, he refused to believe the lies that Satan whispered in his ear. He would believe God's Word. One day, through Jesus, Hope would dance again for joy. She would raise her hands in praise to their Savior instead of cowering to the evil lurking in the darkness. He had to believe that and cling with all his might to those promises. It was the only way he could get through days like today.

Tyler knocked softly. "Honey, can I come in?"

He took her silence as a yes. There'd been many a time when she'd made it quite clear how much she wanted to be left alone.

He tried the door, his spirits lifting as it clicked open.

Inside the bathroom, Hope sat against the wall in front of the basins, knees clutched to her chest. Head buried in her arms, her dark hair hid her face. In one hand, she clutched something. A thermometer? Did she feel unwell, besides the depression which no doubt had already made landfall? Would today be a Category 1 kind of day, or would Hope's meltdown be one of epic proportions, her internal turmoil escalating to a Category 5?

Tyler clicked the door shut behind him—Hope felt safer that way until he managed to calm her—and went to sit down beside her. His gaze focused on her hands, and then it came to him. The date. Of course. The pregnancy test.

He drew a deep breath, his mind spinning, yet at the same time blank. He never quite knew the right thing to do or say in these situations. What could be perfect one time, was disastrous another.

"It's a cloudy day, I know," he started with a whisper.

Without lifting her head, she nodded.

"And cloudy days bring rain." Tyler slid his arm around her. "Henry Longfellow, the poet, said that the best thing one can do when it's raining is to just let it rain. So, honey, you cry all you want because today is a day for us to remember. Today is a day for us to cry. Together."

His voice trembled and his eyes filled with tears. "A year ago we held that pregnancy test, excited beyond measure at the result. And now— Things might not have worked out the way we'd planned, and we might never know why we got pregnant, just to lose our little Matty before he was even given a chance at life, but I have peace in the knowledge that God knows. One day you'll find that peace too, Hope. I believe that because I believe in you. And I believe in us."

Hope's heart-wrenching sobs filled the bathroom. Had he said the wrong thing, again?

How he longed to reassure her that they'd have other children one day, but she wasn't ready to hear that just yet. Instead, he gave a soft chuckle, hoping to take her down a better memory lane. "Hey, do you remember what I said that morning? That we were going to have twins, and you thought I'd misunderstood how a pregnancy test worked. I did get it right, what the blue lines indicated though. We did have a son. And he was perfect. And one day we will see him again in heaven."

He might not be able to make her feel better today, but he'd keep on trying. If she could focus on the good memories, perhaps the bad ones would slowly fade away.

"I love you, Hope, and I know right now you probably don't believe a word I'm saying, but I'm going to say it anyway. I'll never stop loving you, no matter what. I'll always be here for you, ready to pick you up when you're down, ready to laugh with you and cry with you. I'll never leave your side—I'll be right here, cheering you on to wellness."

He reached for her hand.

She didn't pull away as she so often did.

"The day we got married, I made you a promise to love you in sickness and in health. I won't go back on my word, no matter what dark days may come."

No matter how hard it got.

Every morning he prayed for the strength to be able to deal with Hope's depression, for wisdom and understanding, for longsuffering and patience.

Twisting her body toward Tyler, Hope flung her arms around his neck. "I–I'm so afraid. Of everything."

Tyler wrapped her in his embrace. Kissing her head, he whispered, "I know, *ko'u aloha*. I know."

For a long time he just held her, not saying a word as they wept together.

When their tears finally subsided, Tyler placed a finger beneath Hope's chin and eased her head up. He brushed the damp hair from her cheeks and tucked the locks behind her ears.

Red, swollen eyes stared blankly at him.

A distraction—that's what they needed. Something to get her mind off what today was and focus on something happier.

"Do you realize it's only another three months to Christmas? And didn't I promise you a Christmas in Hawaii this year with your family?"

Tiny lines formed between her eyes and on her brow. "Y–you still want to go?"

He smiled. "Absolutely."

Christmas between the walls of their home, surrounded by the knowledge that it would've been Matty's first Christmas making those walls close in tighter, was not an idea he relished for either Hope or himself. They needed to get away.

"All right," Hope said softly. "If you think it's a good idea…"

CHAPTER SIXTEEN

TYLER SET his morning coffee down on his desk and got comfortable in his chair. He powered up his laptop, ready to tackle the new problems that had arisen with the AUV. Between Tyler and his team, they'd been sorting out one issue after the next with this autonomous underwater vehicle. For over a year already! Was this project doomed to sink? He chuckled to himself at the pun. Building an underwater vehicle, sinking certainly was what they needed. Now if they could only get the robot to do what it was designed to do while down there.

His screen brightened and an image of Hope and him on Waikiki beach filled the space. Their holiday in Hawaii over Christmas and New Year had done them both the world of good. Maybe, just maybe, tomorrow's milestone wouldn't be half as terrifying as he'd thought it would be just a few weeks ago.

One year since their worst nightmare had begun. Twelve months since he'd gotten that phone call that changed everything. Three hundred and sixty-five days since they'd lost their beautiful baby boy.

He shifted his attention back to the smiling image staring back at him. Hope seemed happier after visiting her family and the island she loved so much. Had the beauty of the place, being with her parents and siblings, and going down to the beach every day to swim and snorkel in *ka moana* been just what she'd needed to heal? He could only hope and pray it was.

A light knock sounded at Tyler's office door, and he glanced up as Greg strolled in, wearing a wide smile.

"Morning, boss."

Tyler tipped his head. "Good morning. I hope that smile means you've got some good news for me. I sure could use it."

Greg pulled up a chair and sat down on the opposite side of the desk. He leaned forward, excitement plastering his face. "I think we've figured out what's been going wrong."

Until the next time something goes belly up. But, like any problem in life, his team needed to tackle one bug at a time.

Tyler flashed him a smile. "That's what I like to hear. We'll get there, right?"

"For sure."

The chair creaked as Tyler leaned back and folded his arms. "So, you want to fill me in on the details?"

"In a moment." Greg opened his mouth then shut it.

Had he wanted to say something then thought better of it?

"What is it?" Tyler asked.

Greg inhaled deeply. "I don't want you to think I'm prying, but I know tomorrow won't be an easy day for you or Hope. I just wanted to let you know that my wife and I are praying for you both."

"Thank you, Greg. I appreciate that. Actually, Hope has been coping rather well over the past few weeks, so although I know tomorrow will be difficult, I'm hoping it won't be too traumatic for either of us. Nevertheless, prayers are always needed and welcome."

Snapping his fingers, Greg pointed at Tyler. "Hey, you know what you should do? You should take the day off and spend it with Hope. I can keep the ship afloat here."

If there was anyone Tyler would trust to run the department in his absence, it was Greg. But taking time off tomorrow was impossible.

He skewed his mouth downward. "I wish I could. Unfortunately, there's a board meeting in the morning that I can't miss. Investors are getting antsy over how long the AUV is taking to design. I need to give them a full report back on the latest setbacks, with a projection of when a working prototype will be ready."

"That's too bad. I'd take your place if I could."

Tyler chuckled and shook his head. "Believe me, you don't want to be at that meeting, in the direct line of fire."

Greg's laughter mingled with Tyler's. "In that case, I'll make a note to say an extra prayer especially for you."

His laughter subsiding, Tyler grew serious. "I think the best place both Hope and I can be tomorrow is busy at work where our minds can't stray too often to the sadness the anniversary will bring."

Greg shrugged a shoulder. "You're probably right."

"So, do you have anything planned for tomorrow night?" Tyler asked.

"Ha, nope. Judy's cooking something special for us at home, that's all. Do you know how hard it is to get a babysitter on Valentine's Day...I mean night?" Greg lowered his gaze, shifting in his seat. "I–I'm sorry. I shouldn't have said that."

Tyler waved aside Greg's blunder. "Don't sweat it."

Greg nodded, the ruddiness creeping up his neck telling of his embarrassment at his choice of words. "And you?"

Them? He and Hope should have been at home, caring for their nine-month-old son. Instead…

Tyler blinked away the sting in his eyes. "Well, besides the standard bunch of roses and a hearty breakfast, I made dinner reservations for two at our favorite steakhouse. We had planned to dine there last Valentine's, but…"

His gaze filled with sympathy, Greg said, "I'm so sorry for you both. Really, I don't know how you and Hope have managed to get through such a tragedy so well."

If the world only knew.

They'd survived a year, yes. But some days, only just.

Hope woke to the faint aroma of breakfast cooking in the kitchen.

Yum, bacon and eggs.

She rolled over in bed, pulling the comforter over her shoulder and stared at the large bouquet of red roses on her dresser. Déjà vu. Except this time no swollen belly would get in the way of rising from her bed; no tiny kicks would prod from inside her womb. Hopefully Tyler hadn't made plans to take her to the restaurant they would've dined at last year. That was the last place she wanted to be tonight.

All she wanted was to stay at home, spend time in the nursery, and remember Matty.

If only she could turn back the clock.

Hope rose and plodded to the bathroom where she dug out the bottle of tranquilizers she'd tucked away beside the packs of SSRI meds. She hadn't used a tranquilizer in months—didn't feel they'd ever helped much. Even when taking them, she'd continued to feel sad, as if the black cloud followed her wherever she went.

Being home in Hawaii had been good for her soul—not spiritually, but mentally and physically. Although she'd let go of some of her anger toward God in recent weeks, she wasn't quite ready to bridge the gap.

She slid one of the capsules onto her tongue, then filled her mouth with water and swallowed. Fearing the medicine would have the same feeble effect, Hope took another. She wanted to be strong for Tyler today. He was in mourning too, and he'd been through so much dealing with her issues over the past year, she didn't want to make today any worse for him.

After dressing in her work clothes and putting on a little makeup, she grabbed her backpack and slid it over her shoulder. She stole a rose from the vase then made her way downstairs, dumping her backpack at the front door.

Hope strolled into the kitchen, sniffing the air. "Something smells good." She set the rose down on the counter before approaching Tyler.

Glancing up from the stove, he smiled. "You look pretty. Something happening today that I don't know about?" Tyler turned to accept the hug she offered.

"I just wanted to look nice for my husband." She pinched a small piece of bacon from the pan, determined to be in good spirits for Tyler.

"Hey…" he protested.

"It was lonely, sitting there all by itself on the side of the pan, not belonging to any particular strip of bacon." She licked her fingers. "Tastes good."

Pointing to the chair on the other side of the table, Tyler commanded, "Sit. Breakfast will be served in a moment. But first…" He pulled her back into his arms and kissed her tenderly.

"Happy Valentine's Day, my love," he finally said.

Hope poured them each a cup of coffee before she sat down. As she sipped the hot drink, she stared at Tyler over the rim of the cup. How lucky she was to have a husband like him. So loving and caring, not to mention, devastatingly handsome. She didn't deserve him, and she wasn't worthy of his love. That is, if he did *really* love her. Maybe he only stayed with her, tolerated her, and said the beautiful things he did out of pity.

"Are you okay?"

Huh?

Pushing the dark cloud away, for now, Hope nodded. "I'm fine."

"Good. You will let me know if you aren't? Please, honey. I would love to be a mind-reader, but I'm not, and sometimes... Well, sometimes it's just hard for me to tell where your head is."

"I said I'm fine." Her clipped words were uttered in far too much haste.

Stupid.

"I–I'm sorry, Tyler. I didn't mean to be so abrupt. I think I'm just hungry, so I'm getting a little grumpy."

"It's all right." So he said, but his smile didn't reach his eyes.

He turned to grab two plates out of the cupboard then began dishing up the food. "I've made dinner reservations for six-thirty tonight. I thought we could get off work an hour or so earlier today and stop by the cemetery to place flowers on the grave. I bought snapdragons and kangaroo paws yesterday."

"I'd like that," she lied. She didn't want to go for dinner. She didn't want to celebrate Valentine's Day. And to be honest, she didn't want to go to the cemetery either.

She feared dark clouds were gathering over that tiny grave.

Hope had no idea how long she sat at the kitchen counter after Tyler left for work, staring into space. She didn't care either. Finally she knew what she wanted to do today. Needed to do.

Snatching up the rose from the counter, she rushed to the front door. She grabbed her backpack and left the house.

Outside and on a mission, Hope broke a few low-lying, slender branches from the willow oak. Soon after, her Jeep tore down Route 19 Alt, heading for the cemetery.

As she drove, one thought pummeled her mind—what was she doing? She should be going to the cemetery later, with Tyler. But she couldn't stop herself. She had to get to the grave. She had to get to her baby, to Matty.

Matty had been buried in the shade of a large tree, and Hope was grateful. So many graves in this cemetery had no shelter from the blistering sun.

Hope pulled the Jeep to a stop nearby. She grabbed the branches and the rose from the passenger seat and ran to the grave, falling to her knees on the grass in front of the low headstone.

"I brought you something, *'o ka'u keiki pēpē*. My sweet, sweet baby boy."

Hands shaking, she arranged the branches in the flower holder beside the headstone, placing the rose in the center of the greenery. "These branches are from the tree outside your nursery window. Your daddy had planned to build you a treehouse in it one day."

Her trembling fingers inched up the headstone, tracing each letter as her tears soaked the granite stone.

MATTHIAS TYLER DANIEL PETERSON
BORN FEBRUARY 14TH 2002
DIED FEBRUARY 14TH 2002
Gift of the Lord
"The Lord gave and the Lord has taken away.
May the name of the Lord be praised."

"My sweet Matty."

Leaning back on her heels, Hope tipped her head back and screamed at the heavens, "Why did you take my baby from me? Why?"

Man, that was rough.

Tyler slid his laptop onto his desk before collapsing into his chair. He palmed his face and rubbed his eyes with his fingertips, giving a long, slow yawn. Meetings exhausted him. Perhaps if the board had realized what day today was, they might've gone a little easier on him. But he didn't need pity, and he'd managed to buy his team one more month's grace to pull this all together and get that AUV working once and for all. But with all the changes his team had come up with, he was certain they would make it on schedule.

Thank you, Lord. You always meet our needs at the right time. You are faithful. If Greg's news hadn't come yesterday, I don't know what I would've told the board today.

Tyler's phone buzzed in his shirt pocket, and he reached for it. Hope's office number illuminated on the screen.

"Hi honey, is everything okay?"

A moment's silence ensued, before a man spoke. "Um no, Tyler, it's not Hope. It's me, Ethan."

Tyler's heart beat faster. "Ethan? I—is everything all right?"

"That's what I need to ask you. Is Hope okay? I mean, I know what day it is today, and—"

"D—did something happen at work with Hope?" Did she have the meltdown he'd feared she would?

"Well, that's just it… Hope hasn't come in to work yet."

The air whooshed from Tyler's lungs. "What?"

"At first I thought you'd perhaps taken her out for breakfast, it being Valentine's Day," Ethan continued. "I didn't want to interrupt you, but, it's already eleven thirty. I figured you'd be done eating by now, if you'd gone out."

"Have you tried calling her?" Tyler could hear the panic rising in his voice.

"Yes. Your home number, her cell phone... She's not answering any, and I'm worried."

"I–I have to go. Thanks, Ethan."

"Wait!" Ethan shouted. "C–can I do something to help? I can't just sit here at the rescue center, worrying, when I could be out helping you find her. That is, if she's not asleep at home."

If Hope *had* taken off somewhere, it would be difficult to drive and search for her or her car.

A dreadful thought crossed his mind, nauseating him. What if she'd had an accident?

He would have to check the hospitals too.

"Meet me at my house in fifteen minutes." Tyler hung up and raced out of the office, an ominous familiarity overwhelming him.

CHAPTER SEVENTEEN

HOPE'S EYES flickered open. What was she doing here at the grave? Now? She was supposed to come here later with Tyler.

She pushed away from the hard stone she clung to, and her gaze snapped to the strange bouquet of willow oak leaves and the single rose. Shouldn't those have been snapdragons and kangaroo paws, the strange choice of flowers Tyler loved to place on the grave?

She shoved to her feet. "I–I'm sorry, Matty. Mommy has to g–go."

Swirling around, Hope fled from her child's burial place. She had to get out of there. Find some peace. Somewhere.

Hope turned the key in the ignition and the Jeep roared to life. She rammed the shift lever into first gear. The tires spun on the asphalt as she raced out of the cemetery. How very tired she was of acting as if all was well. All was not well, and it never would be. She just wanted peace. Forever. And she knew exactly where she could find it.

At the bottom of the ocean.

Ka moana beckoned her. She had to listen to its voice.

The traffic heavy, it took Hope almost an hour to drive to Pass-

A-Grille. She pulled into an empty parking spot at the end of the street. In front of her, a narrow, sandy path led to the beach and jetty.

She dug in her backpack for her cell phone and turned it to silent, ignoring all the missed calls logged on the screen. Then she threw it inside the glove compartment. She'd had enough of its constant ringing on her trip down south. She no longer wanted to be disturbed.

She glanced at the backpack on the passenger seat, then snatched it up again and dumped the contents onto the seat. The lunch box Tyler had packed for her tumbled onto the floor while her stethoscope snaked across the leather seat before sliding over the edge too.

Frustration boiled within her as she ambled down the jetty, carefully eyeing the rocks that held the sea at bay, protecting the concrete walkway. Everything was too big. How would she ever carry out her plan?

She wandered off the path and onto the rocks. Perhaps she'd find some smaller stones between the larger ones.

Finding a place to sit where the water just lapped her feet, Hope lowered herself onto a chunk of concrete, weathered and smoothed by the ebb and flow of the ocean. For a few moments she gazed across the azure ocean, smooth as glass except for the waves that gently rolled onto the beach nearby. Further out toward the horizon, the sky had darkened, a sure sign of an approaching storm. But for now, the weather remained balmy—only a light breeze lifting her hair, blowing a few strands across her face.

Spying a stone about the size of her hand, Hope reached for it. Her fingers wrapped around the hard, wet surface, and she glanced around to see if anyone was watching her. Only a handful of fishermen stood at the end of the jetty, their lines cast out to sea. Too focused on landing a big one, none of them were concerned about what she was up to.

Hope lifted the flap of her backpack and placed the rock inside. One down, about nine or ten to go. The heavy, filled bag should give her the weight she sought.

She sat for a while longer before moving to another spot. There she found stone number two, somewhat bigger than the first one. She managed to pry it loose from where it was wedged and sneak it into her backpack as well. Maybe she wouldn't need as many as she'd thought.

While the beach and jetty weren't bustling today, it still took Hope quite some time to cram the backpack. Soon the sun would begin to set and the fishermen would pack up and leave— especially with the winds blowing the way they were. She would be alone out here on the jetty. Just her and *ka moana*.

As the gusts of air grew stronger, one by one the fishermen packed up their gear and left. Just as she'd thought.

Hope pushed to her feet. The wind whipped her hair across her cheeks—this way and that. She smoothed away the tangled, thick strands and tucked them behind her ears. She hefted the heavy bag onto her back then moved to the far end of the jetty. Setting the backpack down beside her, Hope lowered herself onto the empty bench. Only a few die-hard fishermen remained, but soon they'd have to accept defeat as well and call it a day.

Then she could finally find the peace she sought.

Until she was alone, she would spend her last moments gazing across the ocean. She'd loved *ka moana* since before she could walk. Choosing to lose her life in its depths seemed like the perfect way to put an end to her suffering.

After phoning friends and acquaintances, and having no luck finding Hope, Tyler and Ethan drove to the cemetery. As they approached Matty's grave, Tyler's spirits lifted. A fresh bouquet had been placed in the vase. He recognized the willow oak branches and the single rose Hope had held in her hands that morning.

She'd been there. But when? By how long had they missed her?

Ethan patted Tyler on the shoulder as they strode across the grass, back to Tyler's SUV. "We'll find her, Tyler. Have faith."

For the next three hours, they cruised through the streets of Clearwater, checking Hope's favorite places and the beaches. They tried her doctor's and psychiatrist's offices. Finally, they agreed they should check the hospital next.

The ER was one place Tyler hoped he wouldn't find Hope, but he couldn't rule out the possibility that perhaps she'd been involved in a car accident.

That search, too, proved futile.

Walking away from the hospital with zero results, his heart despaired. Head hung low with frustration and fear, Tyler stared at the ground as he headed back to his vehicle.

Ethan strode beside him, silent.

Tyler pursed his lips, breathing in deeply. Stopping in the middle of the parking lot, he turned to Ethan and shook his head. "I–I don't know where else to look. We've been everywhere I can think she might've gone."

"Let's go to the police department—file a missing person's report," Ethan suggested.

"Isn't it too early for that? It's not even been eight hours yet."

"My cousin is a cop in Miami, so I know you can at least log her as missing in the NCIC database. That way, if Hope does anything that would cause a law enforcement officer to pull her over, she'd be flagged as a missing person."

"What are we waiting for?"

An hour later they walked out of their local PD. Tyler had no clue once they'd filed the report how it would be processed or when the police would even begin searching for Hope, but it was definitely the next step they'd needed to take. All he could do now was pray that his wife would run a red light, or something.

"I–I guess we should head back to my place," Tyler said as they slid into the car. He desperately wanted to continue searching, but this was far worse than looking for the proverbial needle in a haystack—it was as if they were searching for a single speck of glitter on Clearwater beach.

"I've taken up enough of your time, Ethan, and we might even find that Hope has returned home already." Although it seemed unlikely as they'd driven past their house several times throughout the course of the day.

Ethan offered Tyler a weak smile. "Let's hope and pray she has."

They drove in silence. Suddenly, Ethan's breath hitched.

Tyler's gaze swerved to the passenger's seat. "What is it? Do you remember something?"

"I–it's a long shot," Ethan said, "but could she have driven south to Pass-A-Grille, where we released Val back in July last year?"

Tyler frowned. "The dolphin? The one who started this nightmare? Why would she go there? Especially after all this time. That was almost seven months ago."

Wait a minute…

"She was there? At Val's release?"

Ethan's eyes widened in surprise. "You didn't know?"

"No. Hope never said a word." Why hadn't she told him?

"As I said, it's a long shot. It's just that… Well, Val's last day at the rescue center—the day Joon's calf was born—Hope seemed to have formed a brief but strange bond with the rescued dolphin mother." Ethan shrugged. "But, eh, you're probably right. It *was* a long time ago."

Was it at all possible they'd been looking in all the wrong places today? Could Hope have driven down to the beach where they'd let the female dolphin go, maybe seeking a glimpse of her? Hoping, perhaps, to commune with her once more? Two kindred spirits, from two different worlds, who had suffered the same loss.

Swerving the vehicle left onto Lakeview Road, Tyler pressed the gas pedal to the floor and sped in the direction of Route 19 Alt.

Please, Lord, let us find her. Please, keep her safe.

The trip to Pass-A-Grille was the longest forty minutes of Tyler's life. They drove down the road alongside the beach, eyes peeled for Hope's black Jeep.

Suddenly, Ethan pointed. "There! At the end of the road!"

Thank You, Jesus.

Tyler's lip quivered, and he clamped it between his teeth. His eyes burned with unshed tears. Trying to keep it together in front of Hope's colleague was taxing.

He pulled into the first parking spot he found and dashed from the car. Passing Hope's Jeep, Tyler peered through the driver's window. Empty. But why were the contents of her work backpack strewn across the passenger seat and spilled on the floor? That was so unlike Hope. She hated a messy car.

He rushed down the sand path, Ethan trailing him. The path split, and at Ethan's instruction, Tyler veered toward the right and the beach where the dolphin had apparently been released.

Wind whipped up the fine, white sand, stinging Tyler's arms and legs. He hopped in pain, turning his back instinctively to protect his eyes. With weather like this, it was no surprise the beach was empty. But Hope was close by, he could feel it.

Tyler swung around to the ocean again.

And the jetty.

At the far end stood a lonely figure, hands wrapped around the railings, back toward the land. He would recognize that slender form silhouetted against the setting sun anywhere, the long, dark hair flailing this way and that as it moved to the wind's every command.

Hope.

He raised his hand to call out and wave to her, then decided against it. Best approach her with caution. He had no idea what they were dealing with here.

Placing a finger to his lips, Tyler tipped his head in Hope's direction.

Ethan raised his gaze and nodded. He took a step forward then paused. "Why don't you go to her alone? I think you'll need the privacy. I'll wait in the car for you—it's miserable on the beach."

"Thanks." Tyler handed Ethan the SUV's keys, then turned and jogged down the beach, his heart about to slam right through his ribcage.

He wove his way through the large rocks, clambering over the last few to get to the jetty. With stealth, he moved down the concrete walkway, until he was almost behind Hope. She seemed so lost in her thoughts, he could probably have made a noise getting to her, and she wouldn't have noticed.

He took the last step to her then softly spoke her name. "Hope…"

She twirled around slowly and with a loud sob, reached for him. She collapsed against his chest.

Tyler tightened his arms around her and let her weep.

When she seemed to have cried all her tears, she glanced up at him. "I'm s–so sorry."

He pressed his lips to her head. "Hey, it's okay. I found you. Everything's going to be fine."

Hope shook her head from side to side, distressed. "No, no, it's not okay. I–I almost—"

He waited for her to continue, his gaze fixed on hers. "Almost what, my love?"

Her gaze flitted from Tyler to her backpack beside the railing, and then further over her shoulder out to sea. "I… If it hadn't been for… S–she saved me. Y–you saved me."

Saved her? What was she talking about? He'd found her, yes. But saved? Wouldn't she have made it home eventually? What happened to her today? Why was she this anxious?

Taking Tyler's hand, Hope turned back to the railing. She pointed out across the ocean. "I–I saw her moments ago. S–she spoke to me. Told me to hang on, to be strong."

"Saw who, Hope?" He hadn't seen a soul on the jetty. "Who did you speak to?"

She cocked her head to the side. "Val."

Tyler shifted his gaze in time to see a gray shape in the distance rising from the surface of the water. The sleek body twisted, returning the dolphin head-first to the water with a loud tail slap.

Hope's breath hitched. "It's her."

"Hope, honey, it's just a dolphin. There are many in Tampa Bay—it's a popular breeding ground."

"No. It was her," Hope insisted. "I know it."

Why did she so desperately want to believe it was the creature who had ruined their lives?

"H–how do you know?" Tyler fought against his exasperation. She'd had him running around the entire day, all communications severed, fearing for her life. And all the while, Hope had been dolphin watching miles away from home.

"Because she was here!" Hope pointed to the water below them. "Right there. I saw the star-shaped scars near her left pectoral fin. She's a fighter that one, a survivor, and she told me I can be one too."

Told her?

116

Well, God had used a donkey before to deliver a message, so it wasn't impossible for Him to have used a dolphin to get through to Hope. Heaven knew not much else was working.

"S–she told me not to do it."

"Not to do what, Hope?" She was making absolutely no sense.

Her gaze dropped to the backpack again.

Tyler's mind flashed back to the mess in Hope's car. What did she have inside there now?

He bent to lift the bag, groaning at the weight. "Goodness, Hope, what have you got inside here? Rocks?"

Squatting down on his haunches, Tyler unlatched the cover and lifted it. Instantly, his heart plummeted, thudding in the pit of his stomach. Nausea rose to take its place.

It all made sense now.

She'd had no intention of coming back home.

CHAPTER EIGHTEEN

SEEING THE realization dawning on Tyler's face, Hope's heart broke all over again. To think of what she might've done to him, how close she'd come to losing everything that mattered to her and putting her husband through yet another senseless tragedy.

"C–can we talk?" She gestured toward the bench.

Slowly straightening, Tyler nodded. "I think we need to." He took her hand and led her to the bench close by.

Suddenly aware of the wind slapping her hair across her face, Hope reached into her shorts' pocket and pulled out the elastic band she always kept there for times like this. She drew her hair back and tied it into a ponytail before leaning against the backrest.

Tyler took her hand once again then turned to her, his eyes searching hers. "What happened, Hope? You seemed to be coping so well this morning."

Oh, where did she begin?

Makuakāne, help me.

The three little words, calling on her Father in heaven, took Hope by surprise. That was the first prayer she'd uttered in a year. But would God help her after she'd blamed Him and shunned Him all these months?

Neither death nor life, neither angels nor demons, neither the present nor the future, nor any powers, neither height nor depth, nor anything else in all creation, will be able to separate us from the love of God that is in Christ Jesus our Lord.

At the beautiful reminder that God still loved her no matter what she'd done, no matter how angry she'd been at Him, Hope began to sob. Great, big, ugly tears. *He* had sent Val to stop her from making the biggest mistake of her life. *He* had made sure Tyler got to her in time.

She leaned forward, chest to her thighs as she wept. "Forgive me…forgive me…forgive me." She repeated the two words over and over.

Tyler's arm circled her, his body pressing against her back so comforting. "*Ko'u aloha*, I forgive you. But I need to understand why so that I can help you."

He thought her request was directed at him? Although she did need to ask his forgiveness too. Even so, without having asked for it, she had it.

Unfurling her body, Hope sat upright. She wrapped her arms around Tyler and buried her head in his chest.

She felt freer than she had in a long, long time, although she had no illusions that she was well again—a long road to recovery still lay ahead, but this time she would stick to the path, stay the course.

Leaning back, she looked up at Tyler. "Do you mind if we talk later? I'm emotionally spent. I–I just want to go home."

Tyler gazed at her, his eyes filled with compassion, and smiled. "Of course."

Standing, he grabbed her backpack, hefting it onto one shoulder.

Hope gave a final look across the ocean and the place that had almost become her watery grave. How beautiful it all looked. The sky was no longer blue. The setting sun had turned both sea and sky a bluish-gray, the twin colors separated by a golden horizon. The sun hovered over the divide, casting a beam of light across the shadowy waters, reminding her that the risen Son had shone a light into her dark world today.

They walked away from the fishing jetty and strolled along the concrete path where Hope had collected the rocks. Halfway back to the beach, Tyler paused. He set Hope's backpack down on the ground, opened it and took out the first stone. He was about to toss it when Hope stopped him.

"Do you mind if we keep those? I–I'd like to build a memorial in our garden…to remind me of what God has done today." She sucked in a deep breath then exhaled slowly, seeking strength for what she was about to confess next. "A–and to remember never to hit rock bottom again."

By the time Tyler and Hope returned to the SUV, Ethan had fallen asleep on the back seat. He woke as Tyler helped Hope into the front passenger seat, and released a long, loud yawn.

"Everything okay?" he asked.

Hope started. She whipped her head around to look behind her. "Ethan, what are you doing here?"

"Ethan has been helping me to look for you," Tyler explained as he leaned into the cabin to fasten Hope's safety belt.

"I–I'm glad we found you, Hope," Ethan said as he opened the door and climbed out. "I'll see you on Monday."

Standing beside Tyler, he indicated that he needed the keys to Hope's Jeep.

"Oh yes," Tyler whispered. Logical that someone needed to drive the vehicle back home.

He closed Hope's door then squatted next to the backpack,

feeling for the keys in the side pocket where she normally kept them. Yes, they were there! Tyler retrieved the keys and handed them to Ethan.

He patted Ethan on the back. "Thanks for your help. I don't want to think of what might've happened if you hadn't thought to come here."

"Anytime." Ethan jogged down the road to the Jeep as Tyler walked around to the driver's side of the SUV and slid inside.

"H–how could you bring him here?" Hope's eyes glistened with tears. "This is so humiliating. How can I ever return to work now?"

"Honey, Ethan will be discreet. Whatever happened today will remain between the three of us. And what happened out on the jetty, between the two of us only."

"I–I just wish that—"

"Hope, if it weren't for Ethan, I would *never* have found you. He was the one who alerted me to the fact that something was wrong because you weren't at work. And then he helped me to search for you all day long. It was he who suggested we drive out to Pass-A-Grille. And frankly, I think if he weren't with me, I would probably have lost it for fear of never seeing you again.

"So I, for one, am very glad he was here today."

As he prepared their Sunday lunch, Tyler reflected on the weekend's events.

While Ethan had driven the Jeep back to their house, Hope had curled up on the passenger seat beside Tyler in the SUV. Resting her head on the center armrest console, she'd quickly fallen asleep. The day's events had sapped her dry. She'd even slept most of the following day away, and Tyler had feared she'd completely withdrawn into depression's impenetrable abyss.

So when Hope had woken early this morning and told Tyler she wanted to go to church with him, he couldn't have been more surprised.

During the service, he'd watched her keenly out of the corner of his eye. Clearly God had started something out there on the jetty with Hope that He was bringing to completion right there inside the sanctuary of Clearwater Chapel. He had to trust that soon they'd see only beauty instead of ashes, even though Hope still hadn't opened up to him about what had transpired on Friday.

And they did need to cross that bridge to be able to move forward.

He opened the oven to check on the chicken he had roasting. Another thirty minutes and they could eat.

Hope ambled into the kitchen.

"Hey, honey, where have you been? Or are you just avoiding the kitchen, leaving the cooking to me alone?"

Standing behind Tyler, Hope wrapped her arms around him, resting her head on his shoulder.

His heart warmed. That felt like the good, old days. Before tragedy had struck.

"I'm here now," she said. "What can I do?"

"Make a tossed green salad?"

"Of course." Hope released him and walked over to the cupboard where the salad bowls were stored. Stretching up on her toes, she retrieved one from the top shelf.

"You didn't say what you've been up to since we got home from church," he fished.

She flashed him a glance from the open refrigerator. "I was in the nursery—praying...thinking..."

Hands laden with lettuce, tomatoes and a cucumber, Hope shut the door. She set the vegetables down on the countertop beside the stove where Tyler busied himself cooking the rice.

Picking up a knife, Hope began to slice the lettuce. "And what I was thinking was… Could we redecorate the nursery? Turn it into another guest room?"

He cocked an eyebrow. "A–are you sure? That's a pretty radical move." One Tyler wasn't sure *he* was ready to make. It almost felt as if they'd be packing Matty away, easing him out of their lives.

"I–I need to, *ku'uipo*. The reminders in that room aren't healthy for me. I know if I'm to get well again, I need to make some major changes."

"Then we'll start this week." Whatever it took to see her completely well again. "You just tell me what you want done in there and what furniture we need buy."

"I'll check out some interior design ideas on the internet this afternoon." She dropped the lettuce into the salad bowl and reached for a tomato. "First thing tomorrow morning, I'll call Doctor Montrose, see if I can get an emergency appointment. Would you come with me? I–I thought it might be better to explain everything to you in her presence where she can give a medical perspective on my meltdown."

Wow! That was a giant leap forward for Hope to want to start talking with her psychiatrist again. "Honey, there's nothing that could keep me away from being there with you. Every session, if that's what you want."

She gave a soft laugh. "There is one other thing I'd like to ask of you…"

"Anything, honey. Your wish is my command."

"I need to empty out my backpack before work tomorrow. Would you like to help me build my little monument in the garden this afternoon?"

A smile spread across his face. "Of course. When I said anything, honey, I did mean anything."

CHAPTER NINETEEN

HER HEART pounding, one eye on the door, ready to bolt, Hope eased down on the edge of the couch in Doctor Montrose's consulting room. All day long, a menacing cloud had brewed in her mind, her bravado and resolutions of yesterday pushed aside by its forward surge.

Sitting beside Hope, Tyler squeezed her hand.

She attempted a smile. If not for him, she probably wouldn't be able to go through with this. She hoped that by talking openly and honestly about the monster ravaging her mind she would find freedom from its clutches.

Making herself comfortable in an armchair opposite them, a file on her lap and a pen in her hand, Doctor Montrose crossed her legs.

Hope studied the pale blue fabric of the psychiatrist's slacks as they draped around the dove-gray, high-heeled shoes she wore. For a woman in her fifties, she was extremely elegant. And rather attractive.

More attractive than you, the whispers began.

Stop it!

Hope groaned silently. *Father God, help me to keep my sanity. Help me to get through these sessions. Help me to be vulnerable, and in that vulnerability, find healing. I'm so desperate to recover the happiness that Tyler and I once shared.*

"Hope, I'm so glad you've come to see me today." Doctor Montrose's voice soothed, like honey sliding down a sore throat.

Hope nodded and mumbled a "Hi."

"And Tyler, it's good to see you again as well." The psychiatrist flashed him a smile.

Tyler returned the gesture. "Thank you for making time to see us on such short notice, Doctor Montrose."

The pleasant exchange fueled Hope's doubts again, the dark whispering in her head growing louder.

"It was important." The psychiatrist turned to Hope. "So, Hope, seems it's been quite a weekend. Would you like to tell me about it?"

Not really.

But wasn't that what she was there for—to get well this time? Best she spoke up.

"I…well, um, I…"

"Take your time, Hope." Doctor Montrose leaned forward and placed a small recorder on the low coffee table that filled the carpeted space between them. "Do you mind if I record our sessions? It will help me with your treatment."

Both Hope and Tyler shook their heads.

"Thank you." She turned on the recorder then leaned back in her chair. "Why don't you start at the beginning? What happened after you woke up on Friday morning?"

"Well, I… I could smell the breakfast Tyler was cooking in the kitchen." Hope offered a wobbly smile. "Bacon and eggs."

"Spoiled girl, that's one of my favorite morning meals. You have a good husband." Doctor Montrose scribbled something in the file.

"What happened next?" Her familiar tone had quickly turned professional again.

"I–I saw the bouquet of red roses that Tyler had bought for me and s–suddenly I was transported to Valentine's Day last year. Except, this time I had no baby bump, no little one kicking me to say good morning." The lump in her throat swelled. Tears trickled down her cheeks, and she quickly brushed them away.

Tyler slid his arm around her. He whispered, "It's okay, honey. You're doing great. I'm so proud of you."

His words shone a flicker of light into her darkness, giving her the courage to continue for a little longer. She prayed she would have the strength to make it to the end of her story.

She shifted her gaze back to Doctor Montrose. "I–I was so afraid of facing the day—"

"Because it was the anniversary of your baby's death?"

"Yes." What other reason would she have? Then again, far too often Hope would wake fearful of what the day would bring. Doctor Montrose knew that from their previous sessions, so her question *was* quite logical.

Hope combed her hair over one shoulder then massaged her neck, trying to ease the tightness in her muscles. She inhaled and exhaled slowly.

Just stay calm, Hope. You can do this. Tyler believes in you. So does God.

"I wanted to be strong for Tyler, so I took out the tranquilizers you prescribed for me last year."

"Uh-huh…" Doctor Montrose lifted papers in the file, perhaps in search of the name of the pills Hope had taken.

"They hadn't been that effective the last time, so I took two." Hope stared at Doctor Montrose, gauging her reaction.

The psychiatrist's brows shot up. "Two?"

Hope nodded. "After that, I dressed and went downstairs. Tyler and I ate breakfast together, and then he left for work."

"She was in very good spirits on Friday morning," Tyler interjected. "That's why I was floored at how the day unfolded."

Uncrossing her legs, Doctor Montrose clasped her hands together and leaned forward. "When a person is grieving, it's quite natural for them to fear the anniversaries and the milestones. But very often, the actual day isn't as traumatic as they'd thought it would be, the reality of their loss hitting them a few days before or after the anniversary. So it's not unusual that Hope might've seemed to be coping well on Friday morning and hit rock bottom by Friday afternoon."

"E–everything became a blur after that," Hope continued. "Once alone, I sat in the kitchen for a long time, just staring into space. Next thing I knew, I had this overwhelming compulsion to go to Matty's grave, despite the fact that Tyler and I had already planned to go later that afternoon, and I really wasn't looking forward to it. I feared the dark clouds that were gathering in my mind."

Tyler raised his hand, as if requesting permission to speak.

Hope paused, giving him the floor.

"I just remembered that Hope seemed a little agitated shortly before I left—snapped at me once or twice. To be honest, I was a little taken aback because not long before we were laughing and joking with each other after she had stolen some bacon from the pan."

Hope clasped his hand, weaving her fingers between his. "I'm sorry, *ku'uipo*."

Tyler shook his head. "You didn't do it on purpose, honey."

"Before I knew what was happening, I'd broken some tender branches off the willow oak and was placing them on Matty's grave. I… I couldn't help myself from going there. It was as if a

127

sinister force spurred me on."

Hope closed her eyes and concentrated on breathing in and out slowly, trying to compose herself. Now for the difficult part of her story. But she had to be strong, she had to tell all in order to set herself free and get the help and understanding she desperately needed.

"The time spent beside Matty's grave—and again, I've no idea how long I was there—was extremely emotional. That's when everything got really doleful and confusing. It was as if I suddenly woke up and didn't know what I was doing there or even how I got there. The darkness had overtaken my mind and urged me to find peace. At the only place I knew I could find it—the bottom of the ocean.

"I ignored the constant ringing of my phone, on a mission to end it all. And once at Pass-A-Grille, I purposefully emptied my backpack and filled it with large stones from along the jetty."

Doctor Montrose scribbled furiously in the file. She looked up at Hope. "What was the purpose of the stones, Hope?"

"To help me sink to the ocean floor and never come up."

Tyler released a soft moan, pressing his palms to his face.

Hope hated hurting him like this, but she knew he wanted to…needed to know the truth about Friday.

"So you were aware that you were about to end your life?" Doctor Montrose asked.

"Yes."

"And have you ever had suicidal feelings before?" The questions kept coming from her psychiatrist.

"Yes. Knowing I couldn't put Tyler through that anguish always kept me from acting on those feelings. I–I don't know why this time was different, why I had no control over stopping myself, why the tranquilizers seemed so ineffective."

Keeping her gaze focused on Hope, Doctor Montrose tapped the end of the pen to the paper she was writing on. "I have a theory, Hope, but I'd like you to first finish your story. Why don't you tell us what stopped you from acting on the compulsion to end your life."

Hope nodded, clasping her hands together. "For a long time, I sat on the bench at the end of the jetty, my heavy backpack close beside me. The afternoon dragged on and the sun sank lower in the sky. A strong wind began to blow, slowly chasing the fishermen away until I was all alone on that jetty. I hefted the backpack onto my back and fastened it to my body. Then I stepped up to the railing. I was about to climb over the metal bars and jump into the water when she appeared."

Doctor Montrose paused her writing and looked up. "Who appeared, Hope?"

Hope glanced at Tyler. Would he, or the psychiatrist, believe her? Already Tyler had seemed skeptical when she'd mentioned it after he'd found Hope on the jetty.

Tyler reached for her hands, covering them with his. "It's all right, honey. Tell Doctor Montrose what you saw, what happened. I believe it was real."

"Y–you do?"

"How can I not believe? I called Ethan and asked about Val. He confirmed the scars you described."

"Val?" Confusion clouded Doctor Montrose's face.

"The dolphin whose stillborn calf we delivered on Valentine's Day last year," Hope explained as tears began to trace her cheeks. "She was writhing, and the blow from her tail caused Matty's death."

Doctor Montrose leaned forward and snatched a tissue from the box on the table. She handed it to Hope. "Take a moment to compose yourself, Hope. I know it's difficult for you to relive all these bad memories, but speaking about them will bring healing."

Hope nodded, but remained silent for a few minutes.

She sucked in a deep breath. "Val rose up in the water in front of me, bouncing her head up and down, making clicking sounds. I– I knew she was trying to communicate with me. Trying to tell me she had overcome the same tragedy, and survived, and was now free in the ocean once again. She'd started over.

"Every time I made any attempt to climb over that railing, she'd repeat the gestures. Finally, I took the backpack off my back, and she swam a short distance away. She kept jumping out of the water as if she was keeping an eye on me, checking that I didn't try putting that heavy pack on again."

"Incredible," Doctor Montrose whispered.

"It was then that Tyler appeared, and I had to wonder whether God had sent Val to keep me distracted long enough for my sanity to return and help to arrive."

Lifting Hope's hand, Tyler pressed a kiss to the back of it. "I believe He did. And I'm so g–grateful." His voice broke and he wept.

"Me too, *ku'uipo*. Me too." Leaning her head on Tyler's shoulder, Hope emptied herself of her sorrows.

When they'd both composed themselves, Doctor Montrose continued.

"Hope, I believe you had a paradoxical reaction, possibly caused by the double dose of tranquilizers."

What kind of a reaction?

"W–what does that even mean?" Hope asked.

"It's when a drug gives the opposite effect to the one usually expected. Because you already had suicidal tendencies but couldn't act on your inclinations, the paradoxical effect of the tranquilizers had you being dysphoric enough to want to commit suicide and at the same time break free from the barriers that had held you back."

Setting the file and pen down on the floor beside her chair,

Doctor Montrose stood. She walked over to the console table nearby. "Water?"

Hope nodded. "Yes, please." Her mouth was dry after all the talking.

Tyler declined.

Doctor Montrose poured two glasses and returned, handing one to Hope. "Let me reassure you that it's not common to have a paradoxical reaction to anti-depressants or tranquilizers, but it can and does happen from time to time." The psychiatrist took a long drink then set the glass down on the coffee table before sitting down again. She retrieved the file and pen.

"S–so now what, doctor?" Concern etched Tyler's face.

"Although depression is like an addiction, the road to recovery can actually be quite simple—antidepressants and counseling. Getting the sufferer onto that road—that's the hard part." Doctor Montrose offered a tight smile as she tipped her head to the side.

"Hope, please discard the tranquilizers. Those were only prescribed initially to get you through the shock of the stillbirth. I'd like to try a different SSRI. But please, stick to taking the medication, even if there are some side effects—they will disappear—just give it time."

Hope slowly moved her head up and down again.

"After merely six weeks when the chemical imbalances in your brain begin to settle, you'll start to feel like a different person."

Six weeks… If only she'd continued for a little longer the first time, they could probably have avoided so much heartache, so many difficult days that they hadn't needed to go through.

Doctor Montrose turned to Tyler. "Please make sure that Hope takes her medicine every day."

"I will," Tyler said. "I promise."

"Good. If the side effects are really severe, Hope, don't hesitate to call me—we'll look at trying an alternative drug. It could take a little trial and error to get you on the right antidepressant. I'd like to see you weekly for at least the next four months. Thereafter, if you're making good progress, we can change to bi-weekly, and eventually monthly. I guarantee that within a few months, you will be a different person, and it will all be worth it."

"H–how long will I need to be on this medication?" Hope asked.

Doctor Montrose rose and walked over to her desk. "Same as the last medication I gave you—at least a year."

CHAPTER TWENTY

STRETCHED OUT on Clearwater beach, Tyler propped himself up on his elbow to gaze lovingly at his beautiful wife as she soaked up the hot August rays. Water droplets still clung to her tanned back from the swim they'd just taken. Behind her, Pier 60 created the perfect backdrop.

He sighed. How good it was to have the same woman he'd married back again. Well, almost the same. He was so proud of Hope. She'd worked extra hard over the past six months to be well again, humbly accepting his help and encouragement on the bad days when she just wanted to give up. Those days were fewer and farther between now. By God's grace, they'd soon disappear completely.

Weekends on their favorite beach were often unpleasantly crowded, so Tyler and Hope had taken the Friday afternoon off instead to celebrate this six-month milestone by relaxing on the white sands, swimming and snorkeling in the crystal clear turquoise water, and then catching an early dinner at the restaurant on the pier.

He leaned over to Hope and whispered in her ear, "What are

you dreaming about, honey?"

Her head resting on her arms, Hope opened her eyes lazily. "Hmm, a white Christmas. Only four more months to go. You do know you'll have to teach me to ski."

He chuckled. "I know. And I will."

The ring of a cell phone interrupted the conversation.

Hope closed her eyes again. "That's yours, *ko'u aloha*."

Kneeling on his towel, Tyler dug in their beachbag for his phone. Who could be disturbing his afternoon off?

Finding the phone, he answered. "Brody, what's up?" It wasn't that often he heard from his brother in Kansas.

"Tyler, are you sitting down? I–I have some bad news."

Tyler's pulse beat faster. He leaned back on his heels. "I am. Sort of. What's wrong?"

Hope's eyes flittered open again. She sat up too, frowning at Tyler, her gaze filled with questions.

"It's Faith," Brody continued. "She's been in a car accident near Denver."

No.

"I–is she—?" He couldn't say it.

Please, Lord, let her be okay.

"She's alive and has been airlifted to the nearest hospital. I'm flying to Denver with Michael—"

"Michael? He's there with you?"

"Yes."

What was their nephew doing at Brody's house?

Brody cleared his throat. "Faith and Charles have been having some problems… I only found out last night, although I suspected something was up when she drove here a couple of days ago with Michael. Early this morning, though, Faith left to go back to Colorado. Michael wanted to stay. Seems our sister and her husband might've worked through their issues. B–but she never made it home."

"Sounds serious if they've airlifted her. I should go to her, but—"

How could he leave Hope now? Yes, she'd made strides in getting well again, but she still had the odd bad day. What if she had one when he was away in Denver? He couldn't take that risk.

"No, Tyler. You need to be there with Hope. You know that."

"Maybe we could both come."

"I don't think that's a good idea. You've no idea how a hospital environment could affect Hope—send her crashing down a merciless memory lane. You can't take a chance of something triggering a relapse. Besides, no doubt Faith will be in the ICU for a while, and with only two visitors permitted, Charles and Michael should have as much time as possible with her."

He was probably right.

"Look, I'm hoping to catch a flight soon. I'll keep you posted. If things are really bad and you do need to come—" Brody's heavy breathing whooshed through the phone. "You know what, let's just cross that bridge *if* we get to it. In the meantime, you get down on your knees and pray it doesn't come to that. I'm not so great in that department."

"I'll definitely be praying," Tyler said. *Starting right now.*

"I have to go. I'll call you later." Brody cut the call.

Dropping his phone onto the towel, Tyler raked his fingers through his hair. Pressing his palms tightly against his head, he released a weighted sigh.

Hope reached for him. "What is it, *ku'uipo?*"

"I–it's Faith. She's been in a car accident."

She stared at him for a moment before speaking. "W–what? You should go to her. I'll be fine." She brushed a hand up and down his calf.

"No, honey. My first responsibility is to you. And if Brody can understand that, Faith certainly will too."

Thankfully he and Hope had decided that part of her healing process would involve being transparent with their family and letting them know about the difficulties they'd been having since Matty's stillbirth. They couldn't do this on their own. They'd tried and realized that they needed the support and prayers of their family and friends. Probably a huge reason Hope had made such remarkable progress in her healing this time around.

"All right. But let's take some time right now to pray for your sister, okay. She's spent many hours on her knees for me. It's time to return the favor." Hope shuffled closer and clasped Tyler's hands. She rested her forehead against his.

"*'O ka Makua lani,*" she began.

Heavenly Father…

CHAPTER TWENTY-ONE

SUNDAY...YES! Hope couldn't wait to get to the morning worship service.

Reaching her hands above her head, she arched her back and gave a long stretch accompanied by a soft moan.

Tyler mumbled something beside her before rolling over. Seemed he wasn't quite ready to wake up.

Leaving him to rest for a little longer, she offered her contented smile to the ceiling. At least God would see and smile back down on her.

Hard to think that barely two weeks ago, they'd taken a final run down the ski slope where they were staying in the Rocky Mountains. And a month ago, they were celebrating Christmas with Faith, Charles, and Michael.

Christmas... Sigh.

She snuggled beneath the covers, her cheeks warming at the memory of the romantic night she and Tyler had shared in their cozy mountain cabin. More than the log fire had burned in their bedroom that night. As it had on many nights during their stay in the Rockies. But that particular night had seemed more special than any other.

She giggled into the sheet.

Oh, they'd had such a wonderful vacation in Colorado—two weeks in the mountains, followed by a week in Fort Collins helping Faith and Charles pack for their big move down the road to neighboring Loveland. Faith still struggled a bit to get around, but there was hope that in time, with sufficient physical therapy, her limp wouldn't be as noticeable. Other than that, she'd recovered remarkably well from her car accident only four months earlier.

That was the power of prayer.

Faith and Charles had rented a cabin in the same resort for a week. Together with Michael, they'd celebrated Christmas and New Year with Hope and Tyler. It was wonderful to spend the holidays with family again.

Maybe by next year, she and Tyler would've healed sufficiently to be able to endure a Christmas in their own home. But they had planned the Christmases in Hawaii and Colorado before their tragedy. And taking both vacations had been healing.

Nausea rising out of nowhere, Hope threw back the covers and dashed out of the bedroom, down the passage, and into the bathroom. Hand clamped tightly over her mouth, she made it to the toilet just in time.

Perspiration dampened her skin as she sat in front of the porcelain bowl, her fingers and palms pressing hard against the wooden seat. Hope wracked her brain to think of what she'd eaten the previous night that could've upset her stomach so.

Nothing came to mind.

The food they'd prepared had been healthy and fresh. Certainly nothing that would have one upchucking the following day.

Could she be…

No way…

But when had her last period been? Was she late?

That's right—two weeks before Christmas. She recalled how ecstatic she had been knowing she wouldn't have *that* to deal with on vacation.

Images of Christmas night flashed like a neon sign. The log fire. The snow outside. The romance. Tyler's skin warm against hers...

Hope scurried across the floor on all fours to the cupboard beneath the basin. Kneeling, she flung the doors open and reached inside, fingers fumbling to find what she was searching for. Soon she pulled out a familiar box—one that had been tucked away back there since the day they'd unpacked the bathroom boxes after moving into their new home.

Her hands trembled as she checked the expiration date. Still good for another five or so months. She had nothing to lose by using the pregnancy test. If it was negative, and her malaise was just a twenty-four-hour bug, Tyler need never know.

But if it was positive...

She pushed to her feet, removed the test from inside the box, then quickly peed on the stick. She set it aside.

Three minutes and she'd know. Hopefully no longer, seeing as the test had been lying in a dark cupboard all this time with the clock ticking closer to its expiration date.

As she waited, Hope wiped her face with a damp cloth. The cool fabric made her feel so much better than she had a few minutes ago, though inside, mixed emotions churned. She was happy. She was excited. And at the same time, she was so, so terrified.

Tyler groaned, stretching his arm across the nightstand in search of the alarm clock to still its screeching. His fingers hit the button, but the sound continued, coming closer.

Coming closer?

That wasn't the alarm clock. That was—

Hope bowled him over in bed just as he started to edge upright.

"*Ku'uipo!*" She squealed again, out of breath.

"Whoa." Tyler wrapped his arms around Hope and offered her a lazy grin before rolling her over onto her back. He held her soft, chocolatey gaze. "Someone is happy this morning."

She gave him the widest smile. "I am! I'm *hāpai!*"

"I know." Wait a minute... "Y–you mean you're *hāpai*, not happy?"

"Both!" She shoved a pregnancy test in front of his face. Two pink lines stared back at him.

"You're pregnant? And it's a girl?"

Hope's laughter filled the room. "No, silly. Just a different brand from last time, remember?"

He did now. She hadn't known which brand to buy that first time, and she'd wanted a backup test in case the first one had been taken too early.

Tyler lowered his head until their lips met in a long, passionate kiss. "I am so happy, my love. So incredibly happy."

He took the test from Hope's hands and rolled onto his back beside her. "But, how do you feel about being pregnant again?"

"I'm excited, *ko'u aloha*. And I'm terrified. But mostly I'm excited."

She bounced off the bed, dragging her pillow along with her. She turned and threw it at Tyler. The pillow hit his head with a dull thwack.

"C'mon, sleepyhead. If you don't get up, we'll be late for church. I can't wait to tell everyone. And this afternoon, we're calling my family and yours."

Tyler's eyes widened. "Y–you want to tell everyone that you're pregnant? Before you've seen your doctor? Before the second trimester?"

"Yes." Hope lifted her sleepshirt and smoothed a hand over her flat stomach. "The sooner we have prayers going up for this little baby, the better."

Tyler rose and drew her into his embrace. He kissed her ear and whispered, "So, do you know when our little one will make an appearance?"

Hope's mouth curved into a beautiful smile. Already she had that pregnant glow he'd loved so much. "Let's just say that when we tell people the baby's due date, they'll probably say something like, 'Ooh, a September baby? Well somebody certainly enjoyed their Christmas celebrations last year.'"

Tyler chuckled. "In our defense, we were on vacation."

EPILOGUE

Saturday, September 18, 2004

TAKING CARE, Hope made her way down the staircase toward the front door. Even though they'd be late if she didn't hurry, she still took one painstaking step at a time as she clung tightly to the bannister. It was impossible to see the stairs beyond her ginormous belly and the long, champagne-colored chiffon of her evening gown. Slowly did it, because the last thing she needed was to fall down this staircase.

Seeing her, Tyler scooted up the stairs, two at a time, meeting her halfway.

"Honey, you shouldn't be navigating the staircase in your condition, wearing that."

"I agree, because one false step and this strapless, crystal-beaded bodice will land up around my stomach, and I'll look like a disco ball." She giggled. "One way of being the belle of the ball, I guess."

"Then why didn't you call me to say you were ready to come down?"

Hope took his hand and clung on tightly as Tyler slid his arm around her waist. "I did call. You didn't come."

"I'm sorry, must have been when I was outside pulling the car into the drive. The less you have to walk tonight, the better. I really wish you hadn't insisted on going—it's way too close to your due date. If we win, Greg could've accepted the award on behalf of the team."

"And miss your big moment? The one you've been working toward for so long? No way."

"We haven't won yet."

"You will. I believe in you, *ku'uipo*." And thank God, they believed in each other.

Hope smiled. "Besides, we've been on labor-watch for the past week, and it hasn't stopped us from going shopping or to church or for walks on the beach. Why should tonight be any different?"

At the bottom of the stairs, Hope paused to catch her breath and to straighten Tyler's bow tie. She gazed into his eyes, soft, warm, and inviting. "You look so handsome tonight. I think you will need to wear a tux far more often."

"And you, honey," Tyler breathed out a sigh, shaking his head as he held her gaze. "You look incredibly beautiful. The dress, the hair, the everything…"

Lifting one hand, Hope cupped her palm against her side bun, pleased with how well she cleaned up from her rescue center T-shirt, shorts, and waterproof shoes. Although she had hung those up not long after she found out she was pregnant for the second time. Handed the reins over to Ethan. He deserved to run the center. He'd worked hard for it. She only went in on the odd occasion to visit and help with menial tasks, sticking to working with small creatures only, like turtles—small turtles, because those bigger ones had quite a bite on them.

A long time ago, she'd promised herself that if she could turn back the hands of time, she would do it all differently. Now she'd been given a second chance, and she had stuck to her word.

She planted a light kiss on Tyler's cheek. His five-o-clock shadow that gave him the rugged look she so loved, prickled her skin. "Shall we go, before we miss the big announcement?"

Tyler linked his arm in hers then opened the front door. "We should. The chariot awaits my princesses."

Bending forward, he smoothed a hand over Hope's belly and whispered, "That means you too."

Thirty minutes later Tyler had parked the SUV at the Tampa Convention Center. Soon they were mingling with the hundreds of guests who had flown in from far-flung corners of the world for the 25th International Marine Engineers Design Awards. Tyler's team had been nominated for their AUV.

Over dinner, Hope rubbed a hand across her stomach, shifting uncomfortably in her chair.

Leaning closer, Tyler touched her hand and whispered, "Are you okay, honey?"

"I'm fine." She wouldn't tell Tyler about the slight pains she'd been having all afternoon. Braxton Hicks contractions, that's all.

She hoped.

"Seriously, we can go home if you want. Greg can take over in my absence."

Her eyes widened and her jaw dropped. "You really don't want to make that speech, do you?"

"Me?" He palmed his chest before cracking a smile. "You're right, I don't want to. I hate public speaking. And, I haven't prepared anything because I don't think we'll win. Have you seen the designs that have come out of Finland? Sheer brilliance. I think they'll take first place. Probably second and third as well."

"Well I disagree. I think you stand as good a chance as anyone else in this room to take that trophy and the million-dollar funding that comes along with it. Now, eat your food. And while you're eating, give some thought to that speech."

Finally the awards ceremony was under way.

When the team that Tyler thought would win took second place, and their Clearwater team still hadn't featured, Hope just knew that God was going to bless her husband in an amazing way. And he deserved it because he was such a wonderful man, the best husband ever, and he was going to make the most incredible father to their little girl.

Hope was glad they'd decided to find out the sex of the baby this time. They'd had such fun decorating the nursery in shades of pink and white, and had even managed—with that color scheme—to get a beach theme going in their baby's room. After all, there were many pink beaches around the world. Harbor Island in the Bahamas was her favorite and top of her bucket list to visit one day. Three miles of soft, pink sand.

Glorious.

The emcee's announcement drew Hope back to the present. "...and the winner of the 25th International Marine Engineers Design Awards is..."

Her heart pounded against her ribs.

"Right here from our own neck of the woods, the team from Clearwater Bay Marine Technologies with their ingenious AUV."

A loud cheer rose from around the table as Tyler, Greg, and the rest of the guys representing their team sprang to their feet and fist pumped the air.

Even though Hope didn't think there was a micro-inch of space left inside of her, her heart still managed to swell with pride. Hope was certain she clapped the loudest as Tyler and his guys took to the stage, beaming like her precious bottlenose dolphins.

Tyler took the trophy and held it up high before stepping up to the microphone.

"Ladies and gentlemen, thank you." He breathed out, shaking his head in disbelief. "Wow, what an honor. And what a surprise. To be honest, I really didn't think we would win—there are so many ingenious ideas represented here tonight, from all over the world. So I must confess that I only prepared a speech—well sort of prepared—over dinner. It was during the entrees when my wife reminded me that our team stood as good a chance as anyone else in this room. That reminded me of something else she'd said earlier this evening before we left home. She said, 'I believe in you, *ku'uipo*,' which is Hawaiian for sweetheart, not cupid as some of you might be thinking."

Laughter rumbled through the banqueting hall. When it subsided, Tyler continued.

"Two and a half years ago, my wife and I lost our little boy. Hope was only twenty-eight weeks pregnant. We called him Matty.

"In the months that followed, Hope and I plummeted to depths we never thought possible. When we'd finally sunk to the deepest depth, there was nowhere to go but up. After a long battle, and by the grace of God and the prayers of our family and friends, we made it back to the surface where healing could take place. In fact, the birth of our little girl is imminent."

Tyler held his hand out across the audience in Hope's direction. "Honey, why don't you stand up and show everyone how gorgeous a pregnant survivor can look?"

Hope glanced around the room, wondering if she could just slide under the table and hide there until Tyler had finished his speech, which, by the way, was pretty brilliant so far.

People clapped. And clapped. And clapped.

Finally, Hope relented and rose from her chair. It would be good to stretch her legs, back, and tummy a bit anyway.

"Isn't she just the belle of the ball, folks?"

Oh Tyler, stop now.

Hope chuckled, imagining this disco ball hanging above everyone, casting tiny reflections across the audience…and looking a whole lot like her.

More clapping ensued, even louder this time.

"*Aloha au iā'oe i ka nui o ka meli,*" Tyler whispered into the microphone. He grinned, one hand clutching the mic stand, the other holding the silver trophy. "That one, ladies and gents, is for me and Hope to know, and for you to find out."

A smile curved Hope's mouth.

I love you too, honey.

As Hope moved to sit down, she felt a popping sensation, and then a slow trickle of fluid down her legs.

Oh no!

She wanted to flee the room, but she couldn't. She'd miss the rest of Tyler's speech. She couldn't remain standing either. So Hope did the only thing she could and eased into her chair, more fluid dribbling down her legs. Once Tyler was beside her again, she'd deal with the aftermath of her waters breaking—the wet dress, wet carpet, wet chair, plus how to exit the room unnoticed. There was no way she'd give birth right there, right now—was there? These things still took time, didn't they?

"I want to tell everyone here tonight, that if you ever find yourself at the bottom, drowning, with no way up—there is a way. The cross of Jesus Christ provides the bridge, the ladder, the hand to pull you up that you so desperately need."

In that moment, it suddenly hit Hope. This was part of the reason for everything they'd been through. God never hated her and Tyler to put them through such a tragedy. But He desperately loved these people—every single one in the room—and He had provided the platform for His gospel to shine into their lives. One Tyler would never have had, if not for Matty.

"And so, because of mine and Hope's journey to the deepest depths," Tyler continued, "and because our AUV is designed in like manner, going deeper than any other AUV has gone before, our team has agreed that there's no more appropriate name for our AUV than 'The Matty.'"

He held the trophy up high once again. "This one is for you, son."

Hope wiped away the tears that fell. If that was what Tyler had come up with in a matter of minutes, it was probably a good thing he hadn't prepared his speech because she would just be a blubbering mess.

Not that she wasn't one already.

Tyler and the team left the stage to a standing ovation and made their way back to the table. Setting the trophy down between the plates of dessert that had started to arrive, he leaned in to Hope and gave her a kiss.

She gazed up at him. "Great speech, *ku'uipo*. I'm so proud of you."

Pulling Tyler closer, Hope whispered in his ear, "We need to go."

He eased back, frowning. "Go? B–but we haven't had our dessert yet." He shot a glance at the decadence waiting for them on white, porcelain plates. "And it's here. Waiting."

"I know. And I'm sorry. But my waters have broken."

"What? When?" Tyler uttered the two words louder than Hope would've wanted.

All eyes around the table snapped to them.

Great. So much for sneaking out.

"Um, could I borrow your jacket?" She wasn't sure how much cover it would provide. Thankfully, the lights were dimmed low, so maybe nobody would notice the wet stain bound to be visible on the back of her dress.

Tyler whipped off his jacket then slid it around Hope's shoulders as she rose.

"Bring the trophy home, will you, Greg?"

"And where are you two sneaking off to?" Greg's grin tattled that he knew exactly what was going on.

"To have a baby." Holding Hope tightly, Tyler scurried her away toward the door.

Halfway to the exit, someone from their table shouted, "They're having the baby! Now! Go Hope! Go Tyler! Go Team Matty!"

Hope's heart overflowed with love and joy as the tiny infant, dressed in her pretty pink going-home outfit, suckled at her breast.

She glanced at Tyler, seated in a chair beside her bed, and smiled. "It's better she feeds before we leave the hospital."

He raised his hands. "I'm not complaining. I'm just sitting here, minding my own business," a wide grin stretched across his face, "and totally enjoying the view."

Hope pressed her lips to their daughter's tiny brow. She whispered, "Leia Alamea Penelope Peterson. Perfect, just like you." Leia means child of heaven, and that's exactly what this day-old bundle of joy was.

Their little Sunday child.

For Leia's second name, they'd chosen Hope's mother's name. *Makuahine* was overjoyed when they informed her of their decision. Despite Tyler's insistence that two names were more than enough, Hope put her foot down. Their daughter would bear his mother's name too.

She raised her gaze to meet Tyler's. "Can we make two stops on our way home?"

"Of course, honey. Where do you need to go?"

She smiled. "You'll see."

Ninety minutes later, Hope and Tyler introduced Leia to her big brother, Matty. Afterward, they made their way across to Clearwater Beach. Tyler held their precious bundle close to his chest as their bare feet sank into the warm, white sand. They strode down the beach to the shore.

As the cool waves trickled closer and then lapped over their feet, Hope took Leia from Tyler's arms. Bending over, she dipped their baby's toes into the water.

Leia grimaced and pulled her legs to her stomach.

Hope and Tyler laughed softly.

With a whisper, Hope prayed a blessing over their daughter's life. "Precious little Leia, may you grow up with a love for *ka moana*, just like your mommy and daddy. May the ocean bring you hours of pleasure and wonder, may it fill your life with special memories.

"But more than a love for the ocean, I pray you will grow up to have a deep love and reverence for *'O ka Makua lani*, our Heavenly Father, because He loves you so, so much. Today, Daddy and I promise that we will teach you everything we know about God and His precious Son, Jesus. Our Savior."

Hope settled Leia back in Tyler's strong arms. Then, sticking her hand inside the pocket of her loose, knee-length dress, she pulled out the frangipani flower she'd swiped earlier from one of the many bouquets they were taking home. She tucked the white and yellow flower behind one ear and began to sway her hips, twirling her hands as she danced the hula while humming her favorite Crystal Lewis song, "Beauty for Ashes".

The dance she'd planned for her husband and daughter had quickly turned into an act of worship to the One who loved her more than life itself. With her hands raised to the heavens, Hope danced and sang as the tide rushed in around her.

From where he stood on the beach with Leia, a safe distance

away from the waves, Tyler called to her, "Just look at you."

Hope giggled and continued dancing as Tyler's voice surrounded her.

"I always knew that one day you would dance again for joy."

Her heart soared. God had been so faithful—to her, and to Tyler.

Yes, there were still times when she feared the depression would return someday—she was only human. But she refused to give fear the victory.

So when those times came, she would lift her head and remind herself of everything God had done for her through Jesus, His Son.

Jesus had bound up her broken heart.

Jesus had set her free.

Jesus had released her from the darkness.

Jesus had comforted her in her grief.

Jesus had given her beauty for her ashes and the oil of joy for her mourning.

And Jesus had clothed her in a garment of praise—He'd taken her spirit of despair.

The Lord has given. The Lord has taken away.

Laughing, Hope raised her hands to heaven as she danced through the water, the incoming waves splashing higher up her legs and wetting the hem of her dress.

May His name be praised forever.

THE END

GLOSSARY

Hawaiian:

'Ae : Yes

Akua : God

Aloha : Hello

Aloha au iā'oe i ka nui o ka meli : I love you so much, honey

Hāpai : Pregnant

He'ohana : A family

Keiki : Child

Ka moana : The ocean

Ko'u aloha : My love

Ku'uipo : Sweetheart

Luau : A feast of Hawaiian food, usually held outdoors and usually accompanied by Hawaiian entertainment

Makuahine : Mother

Makuakāne : Father

Nakine : Hawaiian form of Russian Nadezhda, meaning "hope"

'O ka Makua lani : Heavenly Father

'O ka'u keiki pēpē : My baby child

Pahu : (or pa'u) A traditional musical instrument found in Polynesia: Hawaii, Tahiti, Cook Islands, Samoa, and Tokelau. Carved from a single log and covered on the playing end with a stretched sharkskin, the pahu is played with the palms and fingers of the hand. [Wikipedia]

English:
AUV : Autonomous Underwater Vehicle
Cetacean : Belonging to the Cetacea, an order of aquatic, chiefly marine mammals, including the whales and dolphins
DEFCON : The defense readiness condition (DEFCON) is an alert state used by the United States Armed Forces. The system was developed by the Joint Chiefs of Staff and unified and specified combatant commands. It prescribes five graduated levels of readiness (or states of alert) for the U.S. military. It increases in severity from DEFCON 5 (least severe) to DEFCON 1 (most severe) to match varying military situations.
Dysphoria : A state of dissatisfaction, anxiety, restlessness, or fidgeting
Gen Z : Generation Z or Gen Z, also known by a number of other names, is the demographic cohort after the Millennials (Generation Y). There are no precise dates for when this cohort starts or ends, but demographers and researchers typically use the mid-1990s to mid-2000s as starting birth years. Presently, there is little consensus regarding ending birth years.
Manatee : Any of several plant-eating aquatic mammals of the genus Trichechus, of West Indian, Floridian, and Gulf Coast waters, having two flippers in front and a broad, spoon-shaped tail. Sometimes known as sea cows.
NCIC : National Crime Information Center
Stat : Immediately [Medicine/Medical Informal]

I hope you enjoyed reading *Recovering Hope* If you did, please consider leaving a short review on Amazon, Goodreads, or Bookbub. Positive reviews and word-of-mouth recommendations count as they honor an author and help other readers to find quality Christian fiction to read.

Thank you so much!

Reclaiming Charity (Shaped by Love - Book 3) will release on April 9th, 2019. See The Potter's House Books for more details, http://pottershousebooks.com/

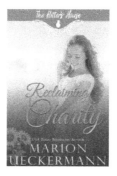

If you'd like to receive information on new releases, cover reveals, and writing news, please sign up for my newsletter.

http://www.marionueckermann.net/subscribe/

ABOUT MARION UECKERMANN

A Novel Place to Fall in Love

USA Today bestselling author, MARION UECKERMANN's passion for writing was sparked when she moved to Ireland with her family. Her love of travel has influenced her contemporary inspirational romances set in novel places. Marion and her husband again live in South Africa, but with two gorgeous grandsons hanging their hats at the house next door, their empty nest's no longer so empty.

Please visit Marion's website for more of her books:
www.marionueckermann.net

You can also find Marion on social media:
Facebook : Marion.C.Ueckermann
Twitter : ueckie
Goodreads : 5342167.Marion_Ueckermann
Pinterest : ueckie
Bookbub : authors/marion-ueckermann
Amazon : Marion-Ueckermann/e/B00KBYLU7C

OTHER TITLES BY MARION UECKERMANN

THE POTTER'S HOUSE
Restoring Faith *(Shaped by Love - Book 1)*
Recovering Hope *(Shaped by Love - Book 2)*
Reclaiming Charity *(Shaped by Love - Book 3 - April 2019)*

A TUSCAN LEGACY
That's Amore *(Book 1)*
Ti Amo *(Book 4)*
Other books in this multi-author series are by: Elizabeth Maddrey, Alexa Verde, Clare
Revell, Heather Gray, Narelle Atkins, and Autumn Macarthur

UNDER THE SUN
SEASONS OF CHANGE
A Time to Laugh *(Book 1)*
A Time to Love *(Book 2)*
A Time to Push Daisies *(Book 3)*

HEART OF ENGLAND
SEVEN SUITORS FOR SEVEN SISTERS
A Match for Magnolia *(Book 1)*
A Romance for Rose *(Book 2)*
A Hero for Heather *(Book 3)*
A Husband for Holly *(Book 4)*
A Courtship for Clover *(Book 5)*
A Love for Lily *(Book 6 - Releasing 2019)*
A Proposal for Poppy *(Book 7 - Releasing 2019)*

HEART OF AFRICA
Orphaned Hearts
The Other You

HEART OF IRELAND
Spring's Promise

HEART OF AUSTRALIA
Melbourne Memories

HEART OF CHRISTMAS
Poles Apart
Ginger & Brad's House

PASSPORT TO ROMANCE
Helsinki Sunrise
Oslo Overtures
Glasgow Grace

ACFW WRITERS ON THE STORM
SHORT STORY CONTEST WINNERS ANTHOLOGY
Dancing Up A Storm ~ *Dancing In The Rain*

NON-FICTION
Bush Tails
(Humorous & True Short Story Trophies of my Bushveld Escapades
as told by Percival Robert Morrison)

POETRY

GLIMPSES THROUGH POETRY
My Father's Hand
My Savior's Touch
My Colorful Life

WORDS RIPE FOR THE PICKING
Fruit of the Rhyme

When love grows cold and vows forgotten, can faith be restored?

Charles and Faith Young are numbers people. While Charles spends his days in a fancy Fort Collins office number crunching, Faith teaches math to the students of Colorado High. Married for sixteen years, Charles and Faith both know unequivocally that one plus one should never equal three.

When blame becomes the order of the day in the Young household for their failing marriage—blaming each other, blaming themselves—Charles and Faith each search for answers why the flame of love no longer burns brightly. In their efforts, one takes comfort from another a step too far. One chooses not to get mad, but to get even.

Dying love is a slow burn. Is it too late for Charles and Faith to fan the embers and make love rise once again from the ashes of their broken marriage? Can they find their first love again—for each other, and for God?

For thirty years, Brian and Elizabeth Dunham have served on the mission field. Unable to have children of their own, they've been a father and mother to countless orphans in six African countries. When an unexpected beach-house inheritance and a lung disease diagnosis coincide, they realize that perhaps God is telling them it's time to retire.

At sixty, Elizabeth is past child-bearing age. She'd long ago given up wondering whether this would be the month she would conceive. But when her best friend and neighbor jokes that Elizabeth's sudden fatigue and nausea are symptoms of pregnancy, Elizabeth finds herself walking that familiar and unwanted road again, wondering if God is pulling an Abraham and Sarah on her and Brian.

The mere notion has questions flooding Elizabeth's mind. If she were miraculously pregnant, would they have the stamina to raise a child in their golden years? Especially with Brian's health issues. And the child? Would it be healthy, or would it go through life struggling with some kind of disability? What of her own health? Could she survive giving birth?

Will what Brian and Elizabeth have dreamed of their entire married life be an old-age blessing or a curse?

 Everyday life for Dr. Melanie Kerr had consisted of happy deliveries and bundles of joy…until her worst nightmare became reality. The first deaths in her OR during an emergency C-section. Both mother and child, one month before Christmas. About to perform her first Caesarean since the tragedy, Melanie loses her nerve and flees the OR. She packs her bags and catches a flight to Budapest. Perhaps time spent in the city her lost patient hailed from, can help her find the healing and peace she desperately needs to be a good doctor again.

Since the filming of Jordan's Journeys' hit TV serial "Life Begins at Sixty" ended earlier in the year, journalist and TV host Jordan Stanson has gone from one assignment to the next. But before he can take a break, he has a final episode to film—"Zac's First Christmas". Not only is he looking forward to relaxing at his parents' seaside home, he can't wait to see his godchild, Zac, the baby born to the aging Dunhams. His boss, however, has squeezed in another documentary for him to complete before Christmas—uncovering the tragedy surrounding the doctor the country came to love on his show, the beautiful Dr. Kerr.

In order to chronicle her journey through grief and failure, Jordan has no choice but to get close to this woman. Something he has both tried and failed at in the past. He hopes through this assignment, he'll be able to help her realize the tragedy wasn't her fault. But even in a city so far away from home, work once again becomes the major catalyst to hinder romance between Jordan and Melanie.

That, and a thing called honesty.

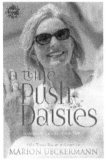

Not every woman is fortunate enough to find her soulmate. Fewer find him twice.

JoAnn Stanson has loved and lost. Widowed a mere eighteen months ago, JoAnn is less than thrilled when her son arranges a luxury cruise around the British Isles as an early birthday gift. She's not ready to move on and "meet new people".

Caleb Blume has faced death and won. Had it not been for an unexpected Christmas present, he would surely have been pushing up daisies. Not that the silver-haired landscape architect was averse to those little flowers—he just wasn't ready to become fertilizer himself.

To celebrate his sixty-fourth birthday and the nearing two-year anniversary since he'd cheated death, Caleb books a cruise and flies to London. He is instantly drawn in a way that's never happened before to a woman he sees boarding the ship. But this woman who steals Caleb's heart is far more guarded with her own.

For JoAnn, so many little things about Caleb remind her of her late husband. It's like loving the same man twice. Yet different.

When Rafaele and Jayne meet again two years after dancing the night away together in Tuscany, is it a matter of fate or of faith?

After deciding to take a six-month sabbatical, Italian lawyer Rafaele Rossi moves from Florence back to Villa Rossi in the middle of Tuscany, resigned to managing the family farm for his aging nonna after his father's passing. Convinced a family get-together is what Nonna needs to lift her spirits, he plans an eightieth birthday party for her, making sure his siblings and cousins attend.

The Keswick jewelry store where Jayne Austin has worked for seven years closes its doors. Jayne takes her generous severance pay and heads off to Italy—Tuscany to be precise. Choosing to leave her fate in God's hands, she prays she'll miraculously bump into the handsome best man she'd danced the night away with at a friend's Tuscan wedding two years ago. She hasn't been able to forget those smoldering brown eyes and that rich Italian accent.

Jayne's prayers are answered swiftly and in the most unexpected way. Before she knows what's happening, she's a guest not only at Isabella Rossi's birthday party, but at Villa Rossi too.

When Rafaele receives what appears to be a valuable painting from an unknown benefactor, he's reminded that he doesn't want to lose Jayne again. After what he's done to drive her from the villa, though, what kind of a commitment will it take for her to stay?

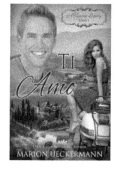

She never wants to get married. He does. To her.

The day Alessandra Rossi was born, her mammà died, and a loveless life with the father who blamed the newborn for her mother's death followed. With the help of her oldest brother, Rafaele, Alessa moved away from home the moment she finished school— just like her other siblings had. Now sporting a degree in architectural history and archaeology, Alessa loves her job as a tour guide in the city of Rome—a place where she never fails to draw the attention of men. Not that Alessa cares. Fearing that the man she weds would be anything like her recently deceased father has Alessa vowing to remain single.

American missionary Michael Young has moved to Rome on a two-year mission trip. His temporary future in the country doesn't stop him from spontaneously joining Alessa's tour after spotting her outside the Colosseum. *And* being bold enough to tell her afterward that one day she'd be his wife. God had told him. And he believed Him. But Alessa shows no sign of interest in Michael.

Can anything sway the beautiful and headstrong Italian to fall in love? Can anyone convince her to put her faith and hope in the Heavenly

Father, despite being raised by an earthly one who never loved her? Will her sister's prompting, or a mysterious painting, or Michael himself change Alessa's mind? About love. And about God.

Womanizer. Adulterer. Divorced. That is Lord Davis Rathbone's history. His future? He vows to never marry or fall in love again—repeating his past mistakes, not worth the risk. Then he meets Magnolia Blume, and filling his days penning poetry no longer seems an alternative to channel his pent-up feelings. With God's help, surely he can keep this rare treasure and make it work this time?

Magnolia Blume's life is perfect, except for one thing—Davis Rathbone is everything she's not looking for in a man. He doesn't strike her as one prone to the sentiments of family, or religion, but her judgments could be premature.

Magnolia must look beyond the gossip, Davis's past, and their differences to find her perfect match, because, although flawed, Davis has one redeeming quality—he is a man after God's own heart.

Rose Blume has a secret, and she's kept it for six long years. It's the reason she's convinced herself she'll have to find her joy making wedding dresses, and not wearing one.

Fashion design icon Joseph Digiavoni crosses paths with Rose for the first time since their summer romance in Florence years before, and all the old feelings for her come rushing back. Not that they ever really left. He's lived with her image since she returned to England.

Joseph and Rose are plunged into working together on the wedding outfits for the upcoming Rathbone / Blume wedding. His top client is marrying Rose's sister. But will this task prove too difficult, especially when Joseph is anxious for Rose to admit why she broke up with him in Italy and what she'd done in the months that followed?

One person holds the key to happiness for them all, if only Rose and Joseph trusted that the truth would set them free. When they finally do bare their secrets, who has the most to forgive?

Paxton Rathbone is desperate to make his way home. His inheritance long spent, he stows away on a fishing trawler bound from Norway to England only to be discovered, beaten and discarded at Scarborough's port. On home soil at last, all it would take is one phone call. But even if his mother and father are forgiving, he doubts his older brother will be.

Needing a respite from child welfare social work, Heather Blume is excited about a short-term opportunity to work at a busy North Yorkshire day center for the homeless. When one of the men she's been helping saves her from a vicious attack, she's so grateful she violates one of the most important rules in her profession—she takes him home to tend his wounds. But there's more to her actions than merely being the Good Samaritan. The man's upper-crust speech has Heather intrigued. She has no doubt he's a gentleman fallen far from grace and is determined to reunite the enigmatic young man with his family, if only he would open up about his life.

Paxton has grown too accustomed to the disdain of mankind, which perhaps is why Heather's kindness penetrates his reserves and gives him reason to hope. Reason to love? Perhaps reason to stay. But there's a fine line between love and gratitude, for both Paxton and Heather.

Holly Blume loves decorating people's homes, but that doesn't mean she's ready to play house.

Believing a house is not a home without a woman's touch, there's nothing more Reverend Christopher Stewart would like than to find a wife. What woman would consider him marriage material, though, with an aging widowed father to look after, especially one who suffers from Alzheimer's?

When Christopher arrives at his new parish, he discovers the church ladies have arranged a welcome surprise—an office makeover by congregant and interior designer Holly Blume. Impressed with Miss Blume's work, Christopher decides to contract the talented lady to turn the rectory into a home. When they begin to clash more than their taste in color, will the revamp come to the same abrupt end as his only romantic relationship?

Despite their differences, Holly resolves to finish the job of redesigning the Stewart home, while Christopher determines to re-form Holly's heart.

Top London chef Clover Blume has one chance to become better acquainted with Jonathan Spalding away from the mayhem of her busy restaurant where he frequently dines—usually with a gorgeous woman at his side. When the groomsman who is supposed to escort her at her sister's New Year's Eve wedding is delayed because of business, Clover begins to wonder whether she really wants to waste time with a player whose main focus in life is making money rather than keeping promises.

Jonathan lives the good life. There's one thing, however, the London Investment Banker's money hasn't managed to buy: a woman to love—one worthy of his mother's approval. Is it possible though, that the auburn-haired beauty who is to partner with him at his best friend's wedding—a wedding he stands to miss thanks to a glitch in a deal worth millions—is finding a way into his heart?

But what will it cost Jonathan to realize it profits him nothing to gain the world, yet lose his soul?

And the girl.

Who am I? The question has Taylor Cassidy journeying from one side of America to the other seeking an answer. Almost five years brings her no closer to the truth. Now an award-winning photojournalist for Wines & Vines, Taylor is sent on assignment to South Africa to discover the inspiration behind Aimee Amour, the DeBois estate's flagship wine. Mystery has enshrouded the story of the woman for whom the wine is named.

South African winegrower Armand DeBois's world is shattered when a car accident leaves him in a coma for three weeks, and his young wife dead. The road of recovery and mourning is dark, and Armand teeters between falling away from God and falling into His comforting arms.

When Armand and Taylor meet, questions arise for them both. While the country and the winegrower hold a strange attraction for Taylor, Armand struggles with the uncertainty of whether he's falling in love with his past or his future.

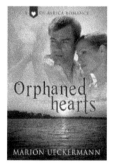

When his wife dies in childbirth, conservationist Simon Hartley pours his life into raising his daughter and his orphan elephants. He has no time, or desire, to fall in love again. Or so he thinks.

Wanting to escape English society and postpone an arranged marriage, Lady Abigail Chadwick heads to Africa for a year to teach the children of the Good Shepherd Orphanage. Upon her arrival she is left stranded at Livingstone airport...until a reluctant Simon comes to her rescue.

Now only fears born of his loss, and secrets of the life she's tried to leave behind, can stonewall their romance, budding in the heart of Africa.

Escaping his dangerous past, former British rock star Justin "The Phoenix" Taylor flees as far away from home as possible to Australia. A marked man with nothing left but his guitar and his talent, Justin is desperate to start over yet still live off the grid. Loneliness and the need to feel a connection to the London pastor who'd saved his life draw Justin to Ella's Barista Art Coffee Shop—the famous and trendy Melbourne establishment belonging to Pastor Jim Anderson's niece.

Intrigued by the bearded stranger who looks vaguely familiar, Ella Anderson wearies of serving him his regular flat white espresso every morning with no more than a greeting for conversation. Ella decides to discover his secrets, even if it requires coaxing him with her elaborate latte art creations. And muffins.

Justin gradually begins to open up to Ella but fears his past will collide with their future. When it does, Ella must decide whether they have a future at all.

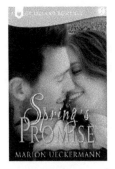

1972. Every day in Belfast, Northern Ireland, holds risk, especially for the mayor's daughter. But Dr. Olivia O'Hare has a heart for people and chooses to work on the wrong side of a city where colors constantly clash. The orange and green of the Republicans pitted against the red and blue of those loyal to Britain. While they might share the common hue of white, it brings no peace.

Caught between the Republicans and Loyalists' conflict, blue-collar worker Ryann Doyle has to wonder if there's life before death. The answer seems to be a resounding, 'No'. His mother is dead, his father's a drunk, and his younger brother, Declan, is steeped in the Provisional IRA. Then he crosses paths with Olivia O'Hare.

After working four days straight, mopping up PIRA's latest act of terror, Olivia is exhausted. All she wants is to go home and rest. But when she drives away from Royal Victoria Hospital, rest is the last thing Olivia gets.

When Declan kidnaps the Lord Mayor of Belfast's daughter, Ryann has to find a way to rescue the dark-haired beauty, though it means he must turn his back on his own flesh and blood for someone he just met.

While Ginger Murphy completes her music studies, childhood sweetheart and neighbor, Brad O'Sullivan betrays her with the new girl next door. Heartbroken, Ginger escapes as far away as she can go—to Australia—for five long years. During this time, Brad's shotgun marriage fails. Besides his little boy, Jamie, one other thing in his life has turned out sweet and successful—his pastry business.

When her mother's diagnosed with heart failure, Ginger has no choice but to return to the green grass of Ireland. As a sought-after wedding flautist, she quickly establishes herself on home soil. Although she loves her profession, she fears she'll never be more than the entertainment at these joyous occasions. And that she's doomed to bump into the wedding cake chef she tries to avoid. Brad broke her heart once. She won't give him a chance to do it again.

A gingerbread house contest at church to raise funds for the homeless has Ginger competing with Brad. Both are determined to win—Ginger the contest, Brad her heart. But when a dear old saint challenges that the Good Book says the first shall be last, and the last first, Ginger has to decide whether to back down from contending with Brad and embrace the true meaning of Christmas—peace on earth, good will to all men. Even the Irishman she'd love to hate.

Writer's block and a looming Christmas novel deadline have romance novelist, Sarah Jones, heading for the other side of the world on a whim.

Niklas Toivonen offers cozy Lapland accommodation, but when his aging father falls ill, Niklas is called upon to step into his father's work clothes to make children happy. Red is quite his color.

Fresh off the airplane, a visit to Santa sets Sarah's muse into overdrive. The man in red is not only entertaining, he's young—with gorgeous blue eyes. Much like her new landlord's, she discovers. Santa and Niklas quickly become objects of research—for her novel, and her curiosity.

Though she's written countless happily-ever-afters, Sarah doubts she'll ever enjoy her own. Niklas must find a way to show her how to leave the pain of her past behind, so she can find love and faith once more.

Opera singer, Skye Hunter, returns to the land of her birth as leading lady in Phantom of the Opera. This is her first trip back to bonnie Scotland since her mother whisked her away to Australia after Skye's father died sixteen years ago.

When Skye decides to have dinner at McGuire's, she's not going there only for Mary McGuire's shepherd's pie. Her first and only love, Callum McGuire, still plays his guitar and sings at the family-owned tavern.

Callum has never stopped loving Skye. Desperate to know if she's changed under her mother's influence, he keeps his real profession hidden. Would she want him if he was still a singer in a pub? But when Skye's worst nightmare comes true, Callum reveals his secret to save the woman he loves.

Can Skye and Callum rekindle what they lost, or will her mother threaten their future together once again?

"If women were meant to fly, the skies would be pink."

Those were the first words Anjelica Joergensen heard from renowned wingsuiter, Kyle Sheppard, when they joined an international team in Oslo to break the formation flying Guinness World Record. This wouldn't be the last blunder Kyle would make around the beautiful Norwegian.

The more Anjelica tries to avoid Kyle, the more the universe pushes them together. Despite their awkward start, she finds herself reluctantly attracted to the handsome New Zealander. But beneath his saintly exterior, is Kyle just another daredevil looking for the next big thrill?

Falling for another wingsuiter would only be another love doomed.

When a childhood sweetheart comes between them, Kyle makes a foolish agreement which jeopardizes the event and endangers his life, forcing Angelica to make a hard choice.

Is she the one who'll clip his wings?

Can he be the wind beneath hers?

Three weeks alone at a friend's summer cottage on a Finnish lake to fast and pray. That was Adam Carter's plan. But sometimes plans go awry.

On an impromptu trip to her family's secluded summer cottage, the last thing Eveliina Mikkola expected to find was a missionary from the other side of the world—in her sauna.

Determined to stay, Eveliina will do whatever it takes—from shortcrust pastry to shorts—to send the man of God packing. This island's too small for them both.

Adam Carter, however, is not about to leave.

Will he be able to resist her temptations?

Can she withstand his prayers?